Five Fantastic Stories

Five Fantastic Stories

©2008 Wilder Publications

Wilder Publications, LLC.
PO Box 243
Blacksburg, VA 24060

ISBN 10: 1-60459-679-1
ISBN 13: 978-1-60459-679-3

Table of Contents

The Stoker and the Stars
by Algis Budrys

Know him? Yes, I know him—knew him. That was twenty years ago.

Everybody knows him now. Everybody who passed him on the street knows him. Everybody who went to the same schools, or even to different schools in different towns, knows him now. Ask them. But I knew him. I lived three feet away from him for a month and a half. I shipped with him and called him by his first name.

What was he like? What was he thinking, sitting on the edge of his bunk with his jaw in his palm and his eyes on the stars? What did he think he was after?

Well ... Well, I think he— You know, I think I never did know him, after all. Not well. Not as well as some of those people who're writing the books about him seem to.

I couldn't really describe him to you. He had a duffelbag in his hand and a packed airsuit on his back. The skin of his face had been dried out by ship's air, burned by ultraviolet and broiled by infra red. The pupils of his eyes had little cloudy specks in them where the cosmic rays had shot through them. But his eyes were steady and his body was hard. What did he look like? He looked like a man.

It was after the war, and we were beaten. There used to be a school of thought among us that deplored our combativeness; before we had ever met any people from off Earth, even, you could hear people saying we were toughest, cruelest life-form in the Universe, unfit to mingle with the gentler wiser races in the stars, and a sure bet to steal their galaxy and corrupt it forever. Where these people got their information, I don't know.

We were beaten. We moved out beyond Centaurus, and Sirius, and then we met the Jeks, the Nosurwey, the Lud. We tried Terrestrial know-how, we tried Production Miracles, we tried patriotism, we tried damning the torpedoes and full speed ahead ... and we were smashed back like mayflies in the wind. We died in droves, and we retreated from the guttering fires of a dozen planets, we dug in, we fought through the last ditch, and we were dying on Earth itself before Baker mutinied, shot Cope, and surrendered the remainder of the human race to the wiser, gentler races in the stars. That way, we lived. That way, we were permitted to carry on our little concerns, and mind our manners. The Jeks and the Lud and the Nosurwey returned to their own affairs, and we knew they would leave us alone so long as we didn't bother them.

We liked it that way. Understand me—we didn't accept it, we didn't knuckle under with waiting murder in our hearts—we liked it. We were grateful just to be left alone again. We were happy we hadn't been wiped out like the upstarts the rest of the Universe thought us to be. When they let us keep our own solar system and carry on a trickle of trade with the outside, we accepted it for the fantastically generous gift it was. Too many of our best men were dead for us to have any remaining claim on these things in our own right. I know how it was. I was there, twenty years ago. I was a little, pudgy man with short breath and a high-pitched voice. I was a typical Earthman.

We were out on a God-forsaken landing field on Mars, MacReidie and I, loading cargo aboard the Serenus. MacReidie was First Officer. I was Second. The stranger came walking up to us.

"Got a job?" he asked, looking at MacReidie.

Mac looked him over. He saw the same things I'd seen. He shook his head. "Not for you. The only thing we're short on is stokers."

You wouldn't know. There's no such thing as a stoker any more, with automatic ships. But the stranger knew what Mac meant.

Serenus had what they called an electronic drive. She had to run with an evacuated engine room. The leaking electricity would have broken any stray air down to ozone, which eats metal and rots lungs. So the engine room had the air pumped out of her, and the stokers who tended the dials and set the cathode attitudes had to wear suits, smelling themselves for twelve hours at a time and standing a good chance of cooking where they sat when the drive arced. Serenus was an ugly old tub. At that, we were the better of the two interstellar freighters the human race had left.

"You're bound over the border, aren't you?"

MacReidie nodded. "That's right. But—"

"I'll stoke."

MacReidie looked over toward me and frowned. I shrugged my shoulders helplessly. I was a little afraid of the stranger, too.

The trouble was the look of him. It was the look you saw in the bars back on Earth, where the veterans of the war sat and stared down into their glasses, waiting for night to fall so they could go out into the alleys and have drunken fights among themselves. But he had brought that look to Mars, to the landing field, and out here there was something disquieting about it.

He'd caught Mac's look and turned his head to me. "I'll stoke," he repeated.

I didn't know what to say. MacReidie and I—almost all of the men in the Merchant Marine—hadn't served in the combat arms. We had freighted supplies, and we had seen ships dying on the runs—we'd had our own brushes with commerce raiders, and we'd known enough men who joined the combat forces. But very few of the men came back, and the war this man had fought hadn't been the same as ours. He'd commanded a fighting ship, somewhere, and come to grips with things we simply didn't know about. The mark was on him, but not on us. I couldn't meet his eyes. "O.K. by me," I mumbled at last.

I saw MacReidie's mouth turn down at the corners. But he couldn't gainsay the man any more than I could. MacReidie wasn't a mumbling man, so he said angrily: "O.K., bucko, you'll stoke. Go and sign on."

"Thanks." The stranger walked quietly away. He wrapped a hand around the cable on a cargo hook and rode into the hold on top of some freight. Mac spat on the ground and went back to supervising his end of the loading. I was busy with mine, and it wasn't until we'd gotten the Serenus loaded and buttoned up that Mac and I even spoke to each other again. Then we talked about the trip. We didn't talk about the stranger.

Daniels, the Third, had signed him on and had moved him into the empty bunk above mine. We slept all in a bunch on the Serenus—officers and crew. Even so, we had to sleep in shifts, with the ship's designers giving ninety per cent of her space to cargo, and eight per cent to power and control. That left very little for the people, who were crammed in any way they could be. I said empty bunk. What I meant was, empty during my sleep shift. That meant he and I'd be sharing work shifts—me up in the control blister, parked in a soft chair, and him down in the engine room, broiling in a suit for twelve hours.

But I ate with him, used the head with him; you can call that rubbing elbows with greatness, if you want to.

He was a very quiet man. Quiet in the way he moved and talked. When we were both climbing into our bunks, that first night, I introduced myself and he introduced himself. Then he heaved himself into his bunk, rolled over on his side, fixed his straps, and fell asleep. He was always friendly toward me, but he must have been very tired that first night. I often wondered what kind of a life he'd lived after the war—what he'd done that made him different from the men who simply grew older in the bars. I wonder, now, if he really did do anything different. In an odd way, I like to think that one day, in a bar, on a day that seemed like all the rest to him when it began, he suddenly looked up with some new thought, put down his glass, and walked straight to the Earth-Mars shuttle field.

He might have come from any town on Earth. Don't believe the historians too much. Don't pay too much attention to the Chamber of Commerce plaques. When a man's name becomes public property, strange things happen to the facts.

It was MacReidie who first found out what he'd done during the war.

I've got to explain about MacReidie. He takes his opinions fast and strong. He's a good man—is, or was; I haven't seen him for a long while—but he liked things simple.

MacReidie said the duffelbag broke loose and floated into the middle of the bunkroom during acceleration. He opened it to see whose it was. When he found out, he closed it up and strapped it back in its place at the foot of the stoker's bunk.

MacReidie was my relief on the bridge. When he came up, he didn't relieve me right away. He stood next to my chair and looked out through the ports.

"Captain leave any special instructions in the Order Book?" he asked.

"Just the usual. Keep a tight watch and proceed cautiously."

"That new stoker," Mac said.

"Yeah?"

"I knew there was something wrong with him. He's got an old Marine uniform in his duffel."

I didn't say anything. Mac glanced over at me. "Well?"

"I don't know." I didn't.

I couldn't say I was surprised. It had to be something like that, about the stoker. The mark was on him, as I've said.

It was the Marines that did Earth's best dying. It had to be. They were trained to be the best we had, and they believed in their training. They were the ones who slashed back the deepest when the other side hit us. They were the ones who sallied out into the doomed spaces between the stars and took the war to the other side as well as any human force could ever hope to. They were always the last to leave an abandoned position. If Earth had been giving medals to members of her forces in the war, every man in the Corps would have had the Medal of Honor two and three times over. Posthumously. I don't believe there were ten of them left alive when Cope was shot. Cope was one of them. They were a kind of human being neither MacReidie nor I could hope to understand.

"You don't know," Mac said. "It's there. In his duffel. Damn it, we're going out to trade with his sworn enemies!

Why do you suppose he wanted to sign on? Why do you suppose he's so eager to go!"

"You think he's going to try to start something?"

"Think! That's exactly what he's going for. One last big alley fight. One last brawl. When they cut him down—do you suppose they'll stop with him? They'll kill us, and then they'll go in and stamp Earth flat! You know it as well as I do."

"I don't know, Mac," I said. "Go easy." I could feel the knots in my stomach. I didn't want any trouble. Not from the stoker, not from Mac. None of us wanted trouble—not even Mac, but he'd cause it to get rid of it, if you follow what I mean about his kind of man.

Mac hit the viewport with his fist. "Easy! Easy—nothing's easy. I hate this life," he said in a murderous voice. "I don't know why I keep signing on. Mars to Centaurus and back, back and forth, in an old rust tub that's going to blow herself up one of these—"

Daniels called me on the phone from Communications. "Turn up your Intercom volume," he said. "The stoker's jamming the circuit."

I kicked the selector switch over, and this is what I got:

"—so there we were at a million per, and the air was gettin' thick. The Skipper says 'Cheer up, brave boys, we'll—'"

He was singing. He had a terrible voice, but he could carry a tune, and he was hammering it out at the top of his lungs.

"'Twas the last cruise of the Venus, by God you should of seen us! The pipes were full of whisky, and just to make things risky, the jets were ..."

The crew were chuckling into their own chest phones. I could hear Daniels trying to cut him off. But he kept going. I started laughing myself. No one's supposed to jam an intercom, but it made the crew feel good. When the crew feels good, the ship runs right, and it had been a long time since they'd been happy.

He went on for another twenty minutes. Then his voice thinned out, and I heard him cough a little. "Daniels," he said, "get a relief down here for me. Jump to it!" He said the last part in a Master's voice. Daniels didn't ask questions. He sent a man on his way down.

He'd been singing, the stoker had. He'd been singing while he worked with one arm dead, one sleeve ripped open and badly patched because the fabric was slippery with blood. There'd been a flashover in the drivers. By the time his relief got down there, he had the insulation back on, and the drive was purring along the way it should have been. It hadn't even missed a beat.

He went down to sick bay, got the arm wrapped, and would have gone back on shift if Daniels'd let him.

Those of us who were going off shift found him toying with the theremin in the mess compartment. He didn't know how to play it, and it sounded like a dog howling.

"Sing, will you!" somebody yelled. He grinned and went back to the "Good Ship Venus." It wasn't good, but it was loud. From that, we went to "Starways, Farways, and Barways," and "The Freefall Song." Somebody started "I Left Her Behind For You," and that got us off into sentimental things, the way these sessions would sometimes wind up when spacemen were far from home. But not since the war, we all seemed to realize together. We stopped, and looked at each other, and we all began drifting out of the mess compartment.

And maybe it got to him, too. It may explain something. He and I were the last to leave. We went to the bunkroom, and he stopped in the middle of taking off his shirt. He stood there, looking out the porthole, and forgot I was there. I heard him reciting something, softly, under his breath, and I stepped a little closer. This is what it was:

"The rockets rise against the skies,
Slowly; in sunlight gleaming
With silver hue upon the blue.
And the universe waits, dreaming.

"For men must go where the flame-winds blow,
The gas clouds softly plaiting;
Where stars are spun and worlds begun,
And men will find them waiting.

"The song that roars where the rocket soars
Is the song of the stellar flame;
The dreams of Man and galactic span
Are equal and much the same."

What was he thinking of? Make your own choice. I think I came close to knowing him, at that moment, but until human beings turn telepath, no man can be sure of another.

He shook himself like a dog out of cold water, and got into his bunk. I got into mine, and after a while I fell asleep.

I don't know what MacReidie may have told the skipper about the stoker, or if he tried to tell him anything. The captain was the senior ticket holder in the Merchant Service, and a good man, in his day. He kept mostly to his cabin. And there was nothing MacReidie could do on his own authority—nothing simple, that is. And the stoker had saved the ship, and ...

I think what kept anything from happening between MacReidie and the stoker, or anyone else and the stoker, was that it would have meant trouble in the ship. Trouble, confined to our little percentage of the ship's volume, could seem like something much more important than the fate of the human race. It may not seem that way to you. But as long as no one began anything, we could all get along. We could have a good trip.

MacReidie worried, I'm sure. I worried, sometimes. But nothing happened.

When we reached Alpha Centaurus, and set down at the trading field on the second planet, it was the same as the other trips we'd made, and the same kind of landfall. The Lud factor came out of his post after we'd waited for a while, and gave us our permit to disembark. There was a Jek ship at the other end of the field, loaded with the cargo we would get in exchange for our holdful of goods. We had the usual things; wine, music tapes, furs, and the like. The Jeks had been giving us light machinery lately—probably we'd get two or three more loads, and then they'd begin giving us something else.

But I found that this trip wasn't quite the same. I found myself looking at the factor's post, and I realized for the first time that the Lud hadn't built it. It was a leftover from the old colonial human government. And the city on the horizon—men had built it; the touch of our architecture was on every building. I wondered why it had never occurred to me that this was so. It made the landfall different from all the others, somehow. It gave a new face to the entire planet.

Mac and I and some of the other crewmen went down on the field to handle the unloading. Jeks on self-propelled cargo lifts jockeyed among us, scooping up the loads as we unhooked the slings, bringing cases of machinery from their own ship. They sat atop their vehicles, lean and aloof, dashing in, whirling, shooting across the field to their ship and back like wild horsemen on the plains of Earth, paying us no notice.

We were almost through when Mac suddenly grabbed my arm. "Look!"

The stoker was coming down on one of the cargo slings. He stood upright, his booted feet planted wide, one arm curled up over his head and around the hoist cable. He was in his dusty brown Marine uniform, the scarlet collar tabs bright as blood at his throat, his major's insignia glittering at his shoulders, the battle stripes on his sleeves.

The Jeks stopped their lifts. They knew that uniform. They sat up in their saddles and watched him come down. When the sling touched the ground, he jumped off quietly and walked toward the nearest Jek. They all followed him with their eyes.

"We've got to stop him," Mac said, and both of us started toward him. His hands were both in plain sight, one holding his duffelbag, which was swelled out with the bulk of his airsuit. He wasn't carrying a weapon of any kind. He was walking casually, taking his time.

Mac and I had almost reached him when a Jek with insignia on his coveralls suddenly jumped down from his lift and came forward to meet him. It was an odd thing to see—the stoker, and the Jek, who did not stand as tall. MacReidie and I stepped back.

The Jek was coal black, his scales glittering in the cold sunlight, his hatchet-face inscrutable. He stopped when the stoker was a few paces away. The stoker stopped, too. All the Jeks were watching him and paying no attention to anything else. The field might as well have been empty except for those two.

"They'll kill him. They'll kill him right now," MacReidie whispered.

They ought to have. If I'd been a Jek, I would have thought that uniform was a death warrant. But the Jek spoke to him:

"Are you entitled to wear that?"

"I was at this planet in '39. I was closer to your home world the year before that," the stoker said. "I was captain of a destroyer. If I'd had a cruiser's range, I would have reached it." He looked at the Jek. "Where were you?"

"I was here when you were."

"I want to speak to your ship's captain."

"All right. I'll drive you over."

The stoker nodded, and they walked over to his vehicle together. They drove away, toward the Jek ship.

"All right, let's get back to work," another Jek said to MacReidie and myself, and we went back to unloading cargo.

The stoker came back to our ship that night, without his duffelbag. He found me and said:

"I'm signing off the ship. Going with the Jeks."

MacReidie was with me. He said loudly: "What do you mean, you're going with the Jeks?"

"I signed on their ship," the stoker said. "Stoking. They've got a micro-nuclear drive. It's been a while since I worked with one, but I think I'll make out all right, even with the screwball way they've got it set up."

"Huh?"

The stoker shrugged. "Ships are ships, and physics is physics, no matter where you go. I'll make out."

"What kind of a deal did you make with them? What do you think you're up to?"

The stoker shook his head. "No deal. I signed on as a crewman. I'll do a crewman's work for a crewman's wages. I thought I'd wander around a while. It ought to be interesting," he said.

"On a Jek ship."

"Anybody's ship. When I get to their home world, I'll probably ship out with some people from farther on. Why not? It's honest work."

MacReidie had no answer to that.

"But—" I said.

"What?" He looked at me as if he couldn't understand what might be bothering me, but I think perhaps he could.

"Nothing," I said, and that was that, except MacReidie was always a sourer man from that time up to as long as I knew him afterwards. We took off in the morning. The stoker had already left on the Jek ship, and it turned out he'd trained an apprentice boy to take his place.

It was strange how things became different for us, little by little after that. It was never anything you could put your finger on, but the Jeks began taking more goods, and giving us things we needed when we told them we wanted them. After a while, Serenus was going a little deeper into Jek territory, and when she wore out, the two replacements let us trade with the Lud, too. Then it was the Nosurwey, and other people beyond them, and things just got better for us, somehow.

We heard about our stoker, occasionally. He shipped with the Lud, and the Nosurwey, and some people beyond them, getting along, going to all kinds of places. Pay no attention to the precise red lines you see on the star maps; nobody knows exactly what path he wandered from people to people. Nobody could. He just kept signing on with whatever ship was going deeper into the galaxy, going farther and farther. He messed with green shipmates and blue ones. One and two and three heads, tails, six legs—after all, ships are ships and they've all got to have something to push them along. If a man knows his business, why not? A man can live on all kinds of food, if he wants to get used to it. And any nontoxic atmosphere will do, as long as there's enough oxygen in it.

I don't know what he did, to make things so much better for us. I don't know if he did anything, but stoke their ships and, I suppose, fix them when they were in trouble. I wonder if he sang dirty songs in that bad voice of his, to people who couldn't possibly understand what the songs were about. All I know is, for some reason those people slowly began treating us with respect. We changed, too, I think—I'm not the same man I was ... I think—not altogether the same; I'm a captain now, with master's papers, and you won't find me in my cabin very often ... there's a kind of joy in standing on a bridge, looking out at the stars you're moving toward. I wonder if it mightn't have kept my old captain out of that place he died in, finally, if he'd tried it.

So, I don't know. The older I get, the less I know. The thing people remember the stoker for—the thing that makes him famous, and, I think, annoys him—I'm fairly sure is only incidental to what he really did. If he did anything. If he meant to. I wish I could be sure of the exact answer he found in the bottom of that last glass at the bar before he worked his passage to Mars and the Serenus, and began it all.

So, I can't say what he ought to be famous for. But I suppose it's enough to know for sure that he was the first living being ever to travel all the way around the galaxy.

Missing Link
By Frank Herbert

We ought to scrape this planet clean of every living thing on it," muttered Umbo Stetson, section chief of Investigation & Adjustment.

Stetson paced the landing control bridge of his scout cruiser. His footsteps grated on a floor that was the rear wall of the bridge during flight. But now the ship rested on its tail fins—all four hundred glistening red and black meters of it. The open ports of the bridge looked out on the jungle roof of Gienah III some one hundred fifty meters below. A butter yellow sun hung above the horizon, perhaps an hour from setting.

"Clean as an egg!" he barked. He paused in his round of the bridge, glared out the starboard port, spat into the fire-blackened circle that the cruiser's jets had burned from the jungle.

The I-A section chief was dark-haired, gangling, with large head and big features. He stood in his customary slouch, a stance not improved by sacklike patched blue fatigues. Although on this present operation he rated the flag of a division admiral, his fatigues carried no insignia. There was a general unkempt, straggling look about him.

Lewis Orne, junior I-A field man with a maiden diploma, stood at the opposite port, studying the jungle horizon. Now and then he glanced at the bridge control console, the chronometer above it, the big translite map of their position tilted from the opposite bulkhead. A heavy planet native, he felt vaguely uneasy on this Gienah III with its gravity of only seven-eighths Terran Standard. The surgical scars on his neck where the micro-communications equipment had been inserted itched maddeningly. He scratched.

"Hah!" said Stetson. "Politicians!"

A thin black insect with shell-like wings flew in Orne's port, settled in his close-cropped red hair. Orne pulled the insect gently from his hair, released it. Again it tried to land in his hair. He ducked. It flew across the bridge, out the port beside Stetson.

There was a thick-muscled, no-fat look to Orne, but something about his blocky, off-center features suggested a clown.

"I'm getting tired of waiting," he said.

"You're tired! Hah!"

A breeze rippled the tops of the green ocean below them. Here and there, red and purple flowers jutted from the verdure, bending and nodding like an attentive audience.

"Just look at that blasted jungle!" barked Stetson. "Them and their stupid orders!"

A call bell tinkled on the bridge control console. The red light above the speaker grid began blinking. Stetson shot an angry glance at it. "Yeah, Hal?"

"O.K., Stet. Orders just came through. We use Plan C. ComGO says to brief the field man, and jet out of here."

"Did you ask them about using another field man?"

Orne looked up attentively.

The speaker said: "Yes. They said we have to use Orne because of the records on the Delphinus."

"Well then, will they give us more time to brief him?"

"Negative. It's crash priority. ComGO expects to blast the planet anyway."

Stetson glared at the grid. "Those fat-headed, lard-bottomed, pig-brained ... POLITICIANS!" He took two deep breaths, subsided. "O.K. Tell them we'll comply."

"One more thing, Stet."

"What now?"

"I've got a confirmed contact."

Instantly, Stetson was poised on the balls of his feet, alert. "Where?"

"About ten kilometers out. Section AAB-6."

"How many?"

"A mob. You want I should count them?"

"No. What're they doing?"

"Making a beeline for us. You better get a move on."

"O.K. Keep us posted."

"Right."

Stetson looked across at his junior field man. "Orne, if you decide you want out of this assignment, you just say the word. I'll back you to the hilt."

"Why should I want out of my first field assignment?"

"Listen, and find out." Stetson crossed to a tilt-locker behind the big translite map, hauled out a white coverall uniform with gold insignia, tossed it to Orne. "Get into these while I brief you on the map."

"But this is an R&R uni—" began Orne.

"Get that uniform on your ugly frame!"

"Yes, sir, Admiral Stetson, sir. Right away, sir. But I thought I was through with old Rediscovery & Reeducation when you drafted me off of Hamal into the I-A ... sir." He began changing from the I-A blue to the R&R white. Almost as an afterthought, he said: "... Sir."

A wolfish grin cracked Stetson's big features. "I'm soooooo happy you have the proper attitude of subservience toward authority."

Orne zipped up the coverall uniform. "Oh, yes, sir ... sir."

"O.K., Orne, pay attention." Stetson gestured at the map with its green superimposed grid squares. "Here we are. Here's that city we flew over on our way down. You'll head for it as soon as we drop you. The place is big enough that if you hold a course roughly northeast you can't miss it. We're—"

Again the call bell rang.

"What is it this time, Hal?" barked Stetson.

"They've changed to Plan H, Stet. New orders cut."

"Five days?"

"That's all they can give us. ComGO says he can't keep the information out of High Commissioner Bullone's hands any longer than that."

"It's five days for sure then."

"Is this the usual R&R foul-up?" asked Orne.

Stetson nodded. "Thanks to Bullone and company! We're just one jump ahead of catastrophe, but they still pump the bushwah into the Rah & Rah boys back at dear old Uni-Galacta!"

"You're making light of my revered alma mater," said Orne. He struck a pose. "We must reunite the lost planets with our centers of culture and industry, and take up the glor-ious onward march of mankind that was so bru-tally—"

"Can it!" snapped Stetson. "We both know we're going to rediscover one planet too many some day. Rim War all over again. But this is a different breed of fish. It's not, repeat, not a re-discovery."

Orne sobered. "Alien?"

"Yes. A-L-I-E-N! A never-before-contacted culture. That language you were force fed on the way over, that's an alien language. It's not complete ... all we have off the minis. And we excluded data on the natives because we've been hoping to dump this project and nobody the wiser."

"Holy mazoo!"

"Twenty-six days ago an I-A search ship came through here, had a routine mini-sneaker look at the place. When he combed in his net of sneakers to check the tapes and films, lo and behold, he had a little stranger."

"One of theirs?"

"No. It was a mini off the Delphinus Rediscovery. The Delphinus has been unreported for eighteen standard months!"

"Did it crack up here?"

"We don't know. If it did, we haven't been able to spot it. She was supposed to be way off in the Balandine System by now. But we've something else on our minds. It's the one item that makes me want to blot out this place, and run home with my tail between my legs. We've a—"

Again the call bell chimed.

"NOW WHAT?" roared Stetson into the speaker.

"I've got a mini over that mob, Stet. They're talking about us. It's a definite raiding party."

"What armament?"

"Too gloomy in that jungle to be sure. The infra beam's out on this mini. Looks like hard pellet rifles of some kind. Might even be off the Delphinus."

"Can't you get closer?"

"Wouldn't do any good. No light down there, and they're moving up fast."

"Keep an eye on them, but don't ignore the other sectors," said Stetson.

"You think I was born yesterday?" barked the voice from the grid. The contact broke off with an angry sound.

"One thing I like about the I-A," said Stetson. "It collects such even-tempered types." He looked at the white uniform on Orne, wiped a hand across his mouth as though he'd tasted something dirty.

"Why am I wearing this thing?" asked Orne.

"Disguise."

"But there's no mustache!"

Stetson smiled without humor. "That's one of I-A's answers to those fat-keistered politicians. We're setting up our own search system to find the planets before they do. We've managed to put spies in key places at R&R. Any touchy planets our spies report, we divert the files."

"Then what?"

"Then we look into them with bright boys like you—disguised as R&R field men."

"Goody, goody. And what happens if R&R stumbles onto me while I'm down there playing patty cake?"

"We disown you."

"But you said an I-A ship found this joint."

"It did. And then one of our spies in R&R intercepted a routine request for an agent-instructor to be assigned here with full equipment. Request signed by a First-Contact officer name of Diston ... of the Delphinus!"

"But the Del—"

"Yeah. Missing. The request was a forgery. Now you see why I'm mostly for rubbing out this place. Who'd dare forge such a thing unless he knew for sure that the original FC officer was missing ... or dead?"

"What the jumped up mazoo are we doing here, Stet?" asked Orne. "Alien calls for a full contact team with all of the—"

"It calls for one planet-buster bomb ... buster—in five days. Unless you give them a white bill in the meantime. High Commissioner Bullone will have word of this planet by then. If Gienah III still exists in five days, can't you imagine the fun the politicians'll have with it? Mama mia! We want this planet cleared for contact or dead before then."

"I don't like this, Stet."

"YOU don't like it!"

"Look," said Orne. "There must be another way. Why ... when we teamed up with the Alerinoids we gained five hundred years in the physical sciences alone, not to mention the—"

"The Alerinoids didn't knock over one of our survey ships first."

"What if the Delphinus just crashed here ... and the locals picked up the pieces?"

"That's what you're going in to find out, Orne. But answer me this: If they do have the Delphinus, how long before a tool-using race could be a threat to the galaxy?"

"I saw that city they built, Stet. They could be dug in within six months, and there'd be no—"

"Yeah."

Orne shook his head. "But think of it: Two civilizations that matured along different lines! Think of all the different ways we'd approach the same problems ... the lever that'd give us for—"

"You sound like a Uni-Galacta lecture! Are you through marching arm in arm into the misty future?"

Orne took a deep breath. "Why's a freshman like me being tossed into this dish?"

"You'd still be on the Delphinus master lists as an R&R field man. That's important if you're masquerading."

"Am I the only one? I know I'm a recent convert, but—"

"You want out?"

"I didn't say that. I just want to know why I'm—"

"Because the bigdomes fed a set of requirements into one of their iron monsters. Your card popped out. They were looking for somebody capable, dependable ... and ... expendable!"

"Hey!"

"That's why I'm down here briefing you instead of sitting back on a flagship. I got you into the I-A. Now, you listen carefully: If you push the panic button on this one without cause, I will personally flay you alive. We both know the advantages of an alien contact. But if you get into a hot spot, and call for help, I'll dive this cruiser into that city to get you out!"

Orne swallowed. "Thanks, Stet. I'm—"

"We're going to take up a tight orbit. Out beyond us will be five transports full of I-A marines and a Class IX Monitor with one planet-buster. You're calling the shots, God help you! First, we want to know if they have the Delphinus ... and if so, where it is. Next, we want to know just how warlike these goons are. Can we control them if they're bloodthirsty. What's their potential?"

"In five days?"

"Not a second more."

"What do we know about them?"

"Not much. They look something like an ancient Terran chimpanzee ... only with blue fur. Face is hairless, pink-skinned." Stetson snapped a switch. The translite map became a screen with a figure frozen on it. "Like that. This is life size."

"Looks like the missing link they're always hunting for," said Orne. "Yeah, but you've got a different kind of a missing link."

"Vertical-slit pupils in their eyes," said Orne. He studied the figure. It had been caught from the front by a mini-sneaker camera. About five feet tall. The stance was slightly bent forward, long arms. Two vertical nose slits. A flat, lipless mouth. Receding chin. Four-fingered hands. It wore a wide belt from which dangled neat pouches and what looked like tools, although their use was obscure. There appeared to be the tip of a tail protruding from behind one of the squat legs. Behind the creature towered the faery spires of the city they'd observed from the air.

"Tails?" asked Orne.

"Yeah. They're arboreal. Not a road on the whole planet that we can find. But there are lots of vine lanes through the jungles." Stetson's face hardened. "Match that with a city as advanced as that one."

"Slave culture?"

"Probably."

"How many cities have they?"

"We've found two. This one and another on the other side of the planet. But the other one's a ruin."

"A ruin? Why?"

"You tell us. Lots of mysteries here."

"What's the planet like?"

"Mostly jungle. There are polar oceans, lakes and rivers. One low mountain chain follows the equatorial belt about two thirds around the planet."

"But only two cities. Are you sure?"

"Reasonably so. It'd be pretty hard to miss something the size of that thing we flew over. It must be fifty kilometers long and at least ten wide. Swarming with these creatures, too. We've got a zone-count estimate that places the city's population at over thirty million."

"Whee-ew! Those are tall buildings, too."

"We don't know much about this place, Orne. And unless you bring them into the fold, there'll be nothing but ashes for our archaeologists to pick over."

"Seems a dirty shame."

"I agree, but—"

The call bell jangled.

Stetson's voice sounded tired: "Yeah, Hal?"

"That mob's only about five kilometers out, Stet. We've got Orne's gear outside in the disguised air sled."

"We'll be right down."

"Why a disguised sled?" asked Orne.

"If they think it's a ground buggy, they might get careless when you most need an advantage. We could always scoop you out of the air, you know."

"What're my chances on this one, Stet?"

Stetson shrugged. "I'm afraid they're slim. These goons probably have the Delphinus, and they want you just long enough to get your equipment and everything you know."

"Rough as that, eh?"

"According to our best guess. If you're not out in five days, we blast."

Orne cleared his throat.

"Want out?" asked Stetson.

"No."

"Use the back-door rule, son. Always leave yourself a way out. Now ... let's check that equipment the surgeons put in your neck." Stetson put a hand to his throat. His mouth remained closed, but there was a surf-hissing voice in Orne's ears: "You read me?"

"Sure. I can—"

"No!" hissed the voice. "Touch the mike contact. Keep your mouth closed. Just use your speaking muscles without speaking."

Orne obeyed.

"O.K.," said Stetson. "You come in loud and clear."

"I ought to. I'm right on top of you!"

"There'll be a relay ship over you all the time," said Stetson. "Now ... when you're not touching that mike contact this rig'll still feed us what you say ... and everything that goes on around you, too. We'll monitor everything. Got that?"

"Yes."

Stetson held out his right hand. "Good luck. I meant that about diving in for you. Just say the word."

"I know the word, too," said Orne. "HELP!"

Gray mud floor and gloomy aisles between monstrous bluish tree trunks—that was the jungle. Only the barest weak glimmering of sunlight penetrated to the mud. The disguised sled—its para-grav units turned off—lurched and skidded around buttress roots. Its headlights swung in wild arcs across the trunks and down to the mud. Aerial creepers—great looping vines of them—swung down from the towering forest ceiling. A steady drip of condensation spattered the windshield, forcing Orne to use the wipers.

In the bucket seat of the sled's cab, Orne fought the controls. He was plagued by the vague slow-motion-floating sensation that a heavy planet native always feels in lighter gravity. It gave him an unhappy stomach.

Things skipped through the air around the lurching vehicle: flitting and darting things. Insects came in twin cones, siphoned toward the headlights. There was an endless chittering whistling tok-tok-toking in the gloom beyond the lights.

Stetson's voice hissed suddenly through the surgically implanted speaker: "How's it look?"

"Alien."

"Any sign of that mob?"

"Negative."

"O.K. We're taking off."

Behind Orne, there came a deep rumbling roar that receded as the scout cruiser climbed its jets. All other sounds hung suspended in after-silence, then resumed: the strongest first and then the weakest.

A heavy object suddenly arced through the headlights, swinging on a vine. It disappeared behind a tree. Another. Another. Ghostly shadows with vine pendulums on both sides. Something banged down heavily onto the hood of the sled.

Orne braked to a creaking stop that shifted the load behind him, found himself staring through the windshield at a native of Gienah III. The native crouched on the hood, a Mark XX exploding-pellet rifle in his right hand directed at Orne's head. In the abrupt shock of meeting, Orne recognized the weapon: standard issue to the marine guards on all R&R survey ships.

The native appeared the twin of the one Orne had seen on the translite screen. The four-fingered hand looked extremely capable around the stock of the Mark XX.

Slowly, Orne put a hand to his throat, pressed the contact button. He moved his speaking muscles: "Just made contact with the mob. One on the hood now has one of our Mark XX rifles aimed at my head."

The surf-hissing of Stetson's voice came through the hidden speaker: "Want us to come back?"

"Negative. Stand by. He looks cautious rather than hostile."

Orne held up his right hand, palm out. He had a second thought: held up his left hand, too. Universal symbol of peaceful intentions: empty hands. The gun muzzle lowered slightly. Orne called into his mind the language that had been hypnoforced into him. Ocheero? No. That means 'The People.' Ah ... And he had the heavy fricative greeting sound.

"Ffroiragrazzi," he said.

The native shifted to the left, answered in pure, unaccented High Galactese: "Who are you?"

Orne fought down a sudden panic. The lipless mouth had looked so odd forming the familiar words.

Stetson's voice hissed: "Is that the native speaking Galactese?"

Orne touched his throat. "You heard him."

He dropped his hand, said: "I am Lewis Orne of Rediscovery and Reeducation. I was sent here at the request of the First-Contact officer on the Delphinus Rediscovery."

"Where is your ship?" demanded the Gienahn.

"It put me down and left."

"Why?"

"It was behind schedule for another appointment."

Out of the corners of his eyes, Orne saw more shadows dropping to the mud around him. The sled shifted as someone climbed onto the load behind the cab. The someone scuttled agilely for a moment.

The native climbed down to the cab's side step, opened the door. The rifle was held at the ready. Again, the lipless mouth formed Galactese words: "What do you carry in this ... vehicle?"

"The equipment every R&R field man uses to help the people of a rediscovered planet improve themselves." Orne nodded at the rifle. "Would you mind pointing that weapon some other direction? It makes me nervous."

The gun muzzle remained unwaveringly on Orne's middle. The native's mouth opened, revealing long canines. "Do we not look strange to you?"

"I take it there's been a heavy mutational variation in the humanoid norm on this planet," said Orne. "What is it? Hard radiation?"

No answer.

"It doesn't really make any difference, of course," said Orne. "I'm here to help you."

"I am Tanub, High Path Chief of the Grazzi," said the native. "I decide who is to help."

Orne swallowed.

"Where do you go?" demanded Tanub.

"I was hoping to go to your city. Is it permitted?"

A long pause while the vertical-slit pupils of Tanub's eyes expanded and contracted. "It is permitted."

Stetson's voice came through the hidden speaker: "All bets off. We're coming in after you. That Mark XX is the final straw. It means they have the Delphinus for sure!"

Orne touched his throat. "No! Give me a little more time!"

"Why?"

"I have a hunch about these creatures."

"What is it?"

"No time now. Trust me."

Another long pause in which Orne and Tanub continued to study each other. Presently, Stetson said: "O.K. Go ahead as planned. But find out where the Delphinus is! If we get that back we pull their teeth."

"Why do you keep touching your throat?" demanded Tanub.

"I'm nervous," said Orne. "Guns always make me nervous."

The muzzle lowered slightly.

"Shall we continue on to your city?" asked Orne. He wet his lips with his tongue. The cab light on Tanub's face was giving the Gienahn an eerie sinister look.

"We can go soon," said Tanub.

"Will you join me inside here?" asked Orne. "There's a passenger seat right behind me."

Tanub's eyes moved catlike: right, left. "Yes." He turned, barked an order into the jungle gloom, then climbed in behind Orne.

"When do we go?" asked Orne.

"The great sun will be down soon," said Tanub. "We can continue as soon as Chiranachuruso rises."

"Chiranachuruso?"

"Our satellite ... our moon," said Tanub.

"It's a beautiful word," said Orne. "Chiranachuruso."

"In our tongue it means: The Limb of Victory," said Tanub. "By its light we will continue."

Orne turned, looked back at Tanub. "Do you mean to tell me that you can see by what light gets down here through those trees?"

"Can you not see?" asked Tanub.

"Not without the headlights."

"Our eyes differ," said Tanub. He bent toward Orne, peered. The vertical slit pupils of his eyes expanded, contracted. "You are the same as the ... others."

"Oh, on the Delphinus?"

Pause. "Yes."

Presently, a greater gloom came over the jungle, bringing a sudden stillness to the wild life. There was a chittering commotion from the natives in the trees around the sled. Tanub shifted behind Orne.

"We may go now," he said. "Slowly ... to stay behind my ... scouts."

"Right." Orne eased the sled forward around an obstructing root.

Silence while they crawled ahead. Around them shapes flung themselves from vine to vine.

"I admired your city from the air," said Orne. "It is very beautiful."

"Yes," said Tanub. "Why did you land so far from it?"

"We didn't want to come down where we might destroy anything."

"There is nothing to destroy in the jungle," said Tanub.

"Why do you have such a big city?" asked Orne.

Silence.

"I said: Why do you—"

"You are ignorant of our ways," said Tanub. "Therefore, I forgive you. The city is for our race. We must breed and be born in sunlight. Once—long ago—we used crude platforms on the tops of the trees. Now ... only the ... wild ones do this."

Stetson's voice hissed in Orne's ears: "Easy on the sex line, boy. That's always touchy. These creatures are oviparous. Sex glands are apparently hidden in that long fur behind where their chins ought to be."

"Who controls the breeding sites controls our world," said Tanub. "Once there was another city. We destroyed it."

"Are there many ... wild ones?" asked Orne.

"Fewer each year," said Tanub.

"There's how they get their slaves," hissed Stetson.

"You speak excellent Galactese," said Orne.

"The High Path Chief commanded the best teacher," said Tanub. "Do you, too, know many things, Orne?"

"That's why I was sent here," said Orne.

"Are there many planets to teach?" asked Tanub.

"Very many," said Orne. "Your city—I saw very tall buildings. Of what do you build them?"

"In your tongue—glass," said Tanub. "The engineers of the Delphinus said it was impossible. As you saw—they are wrong."

"A glass-blowing culture," hissed Stetson. "That'd explain a lot of things."

Slowly, the disguised sled crept through the jungle. Once, a scout swooped down into the headlights, waved. Orne stopped on Tanub's order, and they waited almost ten minutes before proceeding.

"Wild ones?" asked Orne.

"Perhaps," said Tanub.

A glowing of many lights grew visible through the giant tree trunks. It grew brighter as the sled crept through the last of the jungle, emerged in cleared land at the edge of the city.

Orne stared upward in awe. The city fluted and spiraled into the moonlit sky. It was a fragile appearing lacery of bridges, winking dots of light. The bridges wove back and forth from building to building until the entire visible network appeared one gigantic dew-glittering web.

"All that with glass," murmured Orne.

"What's happening?" hissed Stetson.

Orne touched his throat contact. "We're just into the city clearing, proceeding toward the nearest building."

"This is far enough," said Tanub.

Orne stopped the sled. In the moonlight, he could see armed Gienahns all around. The buttressed pedestal of one of the buildings loomed directly ahead. It looked taller than had the scout cruiser in its jungle landing circle.

Tanub leaned close to Orne's shoulder. "We have not deceived you, have we, Orne?"

"Huh? What do you mean?"

"You have recognized that we are not mutated members of your race."

Orne swallowed. Into his ears came Stetson's voice: "Better admit it."

"That's true," said Orne.

"I like you, Orne," said Tanub. "You shall be one of my slaves. You will teach me many things."

"How did you capture the Delphinus?" asked Orne.

"You know that, too?"

"You have one of their rifles," said Orne.

"Your race is no match for us, Orne ... in cunning, in strength, in the prowess of the mind. Your ship landed to repair its tubes. Very inferior ceramics in those tubes."

Orne turned, looked at Tanub in the dim glow of the cab light. "Have you heard about the I-A, Tanub?"

"I-A? What is that?" There was a wary tenseness in the Gienahn's figure. His mouth opened to reveal the long canines.

"You took the Delphinus by treachery?" asked Orne.

"They were simple fools," said Tanub. "We are smaller, thus they thought us weaker." The Mark XX's muzzle came around to center on Orne's stomach. "You have not answered my question. What is the I-A?"

"I am of the I-A," said Orne. "Where've you hidden the Delphinus?"

"In the place that suits us best," said Tanub. "In all our history there has never been a better place."

"What do you plan to do with it?" asked Orne.

"Within a year we will have a copy with our own improvements. After that—"

"You intend to start a war?" asked Orne.

"In the jungle the strong slay the weak until only the strong remain," said Tanub.

"And then the strong prey upon each other?" asked Orne.

"That is a quibble for women," said Tanub.

"It's too bad you feel that way," said Orne. "When two cultures meet like this they tend to help each other. What have you done with the crew of the Delphinus?"

"They are slaves," said Tanub. "Those who still live. Some resisted. Others objected to teaching us what we want to know." He waved the gun muzzle. "You will not be that foolish, will you, Orne?"

"No need to be," said Orne. "I've another little lesson to teach you: I already know where you've hidden the Delphinus."

"Go, boy!" hissed Stetson. "Where is it?"

"Impossible!" barked Tanub.

"It's on your moon," said Orne. "Darkside. It's on a mountain on the darkside of your moon."

Tanub's eyes dilated, contracted. "You read minds?"

"The I-A has no need to read minds," said Orne. "We rely on superior mental prowess."

"The marines are on their way," hissed Stetson. "We're coming in to get you. I'm going to want to know how you guessed that one."

"You are a weak fool like the others," gritted Tanub.

"It's too bad you formed your opinion of us by observing only the low grades of the R&R," said Orne.

"Easy, boy," hissed Stetson. "Don't pick a fight with him now. Remember, his race is arboreal. He's probably as strong as an ape."

"I could kill you where you sit!" grated Tanub.

"You write finish for your entire planet if you do," said Orne. "I'm not alone. There are others listening to every word we say. There's a ship overhead that could split open your planet with one bomb—wash it with molten rock. It'd run like the glass you use for your buildings."

"You are lying!"

"We'll make you an offer," said Orne. "We don't really want to exterminate you. We'll give you limited membership in the Galactic Federation until you prove you're no menace to us."

"Keep talking," hissed Stetson. "Keep him interested."

"You dare insult me!" growled Tanub.

"You had better believe me," said Orne. "We—"

Stetson's voice interrupted him: "Got it, Orne! They caught the Delphinus on the ground right where you said it'd be! Blew the tubes off it. Marines now mopping up."

"It's like this," said Orne. "We already have recaptured the Delphinus." Tanub's eyes went instinctively skyward.

"Except for the captured armament you still hold, you obviously don't have the weapons to meet us," continued Orne. "Otherwise, you wouldn't be carrying that rifle off the Delphinus."

"If you speak the truth, then we shall die bravely," said Tanub.

"No need for you to die," said Orne.

"Better to die than be slaves," said Tanub.

"We don't need slaves," said Orne. "We—"

"I cannot take the chance that you are lying," said Tanub. "I must kill you now."

Orne's foot rested on the air sled control pedal. He depressed it. Instantly, the sled shot skyward, heavy G's pressing them down into the seats. The gun in Tanub's hands was slammed into his lap. He struggled to raise it. To Orne, the weight was still only about twice that of his home planet of Chargon. He reached over, took the rifle, found safety belts, bound Tanub with them. Then he eased off the acceleration.

"We don't need slaves," said Orne. "We have machines to do our work. We'll send experts in here, teach you people how to exploit your planet, how to build good transportation facilities, show you how to mine your minerals, how to—"

"And what do we do in return?" whispered Tanub.

"You could start by teaching us how you make superior glass," said Orne. "I certainly hope you see things our way. We really don't want to have to come down there and clean you out. It'd be a shame to have to blast that city into little pieces."

Tanub wilted. Presently, he said: "Send me back. I will discuss this with ... our council." He stared at Orne. "You I-A's are too strong. We did not know."

In the wardroom of Stetson's scout cruiser, the lights were low, the leather chairs comfortable, the green beige table set with a decanter of Hochar brandy and two glasses.

Orne lifted his glass, sipped the liquor, smacked his lips. "For a while there, I thought I'd never be tasting anything like this again."

Stetson took his own glass. "ComGO heard the whole thing over the general monitor net," he said. "D'you know you've been breveted to senior field man?"

"Ah, they've already recognized my sterling worth," said Orne.

The wolfish grin took over Stetson's big features. "Senior field men last about half as long as the juniors," he said. "Mortality's terrific?"

"I might've known," said Orne. He took another sip of the brandy.

Stetson flicked on the switch of a recorder beside him. "O.K. You can go ahead any time."

"Where do you want me to start?"

"First, how'd you spot right away where they'd hidden the Delphinus?"

"Easy. Tanub's word for his people was Grazzi. Most races call themselves something meaning The People. But in his tongue that's Ocheero. Grazzi wasn't on the translated list. I started working on it. The most likely answer was that it had been adopted from another language, and meant enemy."

"And that told you where the Delphinus was?"

"No. But it fitted my hunch about these Gienahns. I'd kind of felt from the first minute of meeting them that they had a culture like the Indians of ancient Terra."

"Why?"

"They came in like a primitive raiding party. The leader dropped right onto the hood of my sled. An act of bravery, no less. Counting coup, you see?"

"I guess so."

"Then he said he was High Path Chief. That wasn't on the language list, either. But it was easy: Raider Chief. There's a word in almost every language in history that means raider and derives from a word for road, path or highway."

"Highwaymen," said Stetson.

"Raid itself," said Orne. "An ancient Terran language corruption of road."

"Yeah, yeah. But where'd all this translation griff put—"

"Don't be impatient. Glass-blowing culture meant they were just out of the primitive stage. That, we could control. Next, he said their moon was Chiranachuruso, translated as The Limb of Victory. After that it just fell into place."

"How?"

"The vertical-slit pupils of their eyes. Doesn't that mean anything to you?"

"Maybe. What's it mean to you?"

"Night-hunting predator accustomed to dropping upon its victims from above. No other type of creature ever has had the vertical slit. And Tanub said himself that the Delphinus was hidden in the best place in all of their history. History? That'd be a high place. Dark, likewise. Ergo: a high place on the darkside of their moon."

"I'm a pie-eyed greepus," whispered Stetson.

Orne grinned, said: "You probably are ... sir."

Bad Medicine
by Robert Sheckley

On May 2, 2103, Elwood Caswell walked rapidly down Broadway with a loaded revolver hidden in his coat pocket. He didn't want to use the weapon, but feared he might anyhow. This was a justifiable assumption, for Caswell was a homicidal maniac.

It was a gentle, misty spring day and the air held the smell of rain and blossoming-dogwood. Caswell gripped the revolver in his sweaty right hand and tried to think of a single valid reason why he should not kill a man named Magnessen, who, the other day, had commented on how well Caswell looked.

What business was it of Magnessen's how he looked? Damned busybodies, always spoiling things for everybody....

Caswell was a choleric little man with fierce red eyes, bulldog jowls and ginger-red hair. He was the sort you would expect to find perched on a detergent box, orating to a crowd of lunching businessmen and amused students, shouting, "Mars for the Martians, Venus for the Venusians!"

But in truth, Caswell was uninterested in the deplorable social conditions of extraterrestrials. He was a jetbus conductor for the New York Rapid Transit Corporation. He minded his own business. And he was quite mad.

Fortunately, he knew this at least part of the time, with at least half of his mind.

Perspiring freely, Caswell continued down Broadway toward the 43rd Street branch of Home Therapy Appliances, Inc. His friend Magnessen would be finishing work soon, returning to his little apartment less than a block from Caswell's. How easy it would be, how pleasant, to saunter in, exchange a few words and....

No! Caswell took a deep gulp of air and reminded himself that he didn't really want to kill anyone. It was not right to kill people. The authorities would lock him up, his friends wouldn't understand, his mother would never have approved.

But these arguments seemed pallid, over-intellectual and entirely without force. The simple fact remained—he wanted to kill Magnessen.

Could so strong a desire be wrong? Or even unhealthy?

Yes, it could! With an agonized groan, Caswell sprinted the last few steps into the Home Therapy Appliances Store.

Just being within such a place gave him an immediate sense of relief. The lighting was discreet, the draperies were neutral, the displays of glittering therapy machines were neither too bland nor obstreperous. It was the kind of place where a man could happily lie down on the carpet in the shadow of the therapy machines, secure in the knowledge that help for any sort of trouble was at hand.

A clerk with fair hair and a long, supercilious nose glided up softly, but not too softly, and murmured, "May one help?"

"Therapy!" said Caswell.

"Of course, sir," the clerk answered, smoothing his lapels and smiling winningly. "That is what we are here for." He gave Caswell a searching look, performed an instant mental diagnosis, and tapped a gleaming white-and-copper machine.

"Now this," the clerk said, "is the new Alcoholic Reliever, built by IBM and advertised in the leading magazines. A handsome piece of furniture, I think you will agree, and not out of place in any home. It opens into a television set."

With a flick of his narrow wrist, the clerk opened the Alcoholic Reliever, revealing a 52-inch screen.

"I need—" Caswell began.

"Therapy," the clerk finished for him. "Of course. I just wanted to point out that this model need never cause embarrassment for yourself, your friends or loved ones. Notice, if you will, the recessed dial which controls the desired degree of drinking. See? If you do not wish total abstinence, you can set it to heavy, moderate, social or light. That is a new feature, unique in mechanotherapy."

"I am not an alcoholic," Caswell said, with considerable dignity. "The New York Rapid Transit Corporation does not hire alcoholics."

"Oh," said the clerk, glancing distrustfully at Caswell's bloodshot eyes. "You seem a little nervous. Perhaps the portable Bendix Anxiety Reducer—"

"Anxiety's not my ticket, either. What have you got for homicidal mania?"

The clerk pursed his lips. "Schizophrenic or manic-depressive origins?"

"I don't know," Caswell admitted, somewhat taken aback.

"It really doesn't matter," the clerk told him. "Just a private theory of my own. From my experience in the store, redheads and blonds are prone to schizophrenia, while brunettes incline toward the manic-depressive."

"That's interesting. Have you worked here long?"

"A week. Now then, here is just what you need, sir." He put his hand affectionately on a squat black machine with chrome trim.

"What's that?"

"That, sir, is the Rex Regenerator, built by General Motors. Isn't it handsome? It can go with any decor and opens up into a well-stocked bar. Your friends, family, loved ones need never know—"

"Will it cure a homicidal urge?" Caswell asked. "A strong one?"

"Absolutely. Don't confuse this with the little ten amp neurosis models. This is a hefty, heavy-duty, twenty-five amp machine for a really deep-rooted major condition."

"That's what I've got," said Caswell, with pardonable pride.

"This baby'll jolt it out of you. Big, heavy-duty thrust bearings! Oversize heat absorbers! Completely insulated! Sensitivity range of over—"

"I'll take it," Caswell said. "Right now. I'll pay cash."

"Fine! I'll just telephone Storage and—"

"This one'll do," Caswell said, pulling out his billfold. "I'm in a hurry to use it. I want to kill my friend Magnessen, you know."

The clerk clucked sympathetically. "You wouldn't want to do that ... Plus five percent sales tax. Thank you, sir. Full instructions are inside."

Caswell thanked him, lifted the Regenerator in both arms and hurried out.

After figuring his commission, the clerk smiled to himself and lighted a cigarette. His enjoyment was spoiled when the manager, a large man impressively equipped with pince-nez, marched out of his office.

"Haskins," the manager said, "I thought I asked you to rid yourself of that filthy habit."

"Yes, Mr. Follansby, sorry, sir," Haskins apologized, snubbing out the cigarette. "I'll use the display Denicotinizer at once. Made rather a good sale, Mr. Follansby. One of the big Rex Regenerators."

"Really?" said the manager, impressed. "It isn't often we—wait a minute! You didn't sell the floor model, did you?"

"Why—why, I'm afraid I did, Mr. Follansby. The customer was in such a terrible hurry. Was there any reason—"

Mr. Follansby gripped his prominent white forehead in both hands, as though he wished to rip it off. "Haskins, I told you. I must have told you! That display Regenerator was a Martian model. For giving mechanotherapy to Martians."

"Oh," Haskins said. He thought for a moment. "Oh."

Mr. Follansby stared at his clerk in grim silence.

"But does it really matter?" Haskins asked quickly. "Surely the machine won't discriminate. I should think it would treat a homicidal tendency even if the patient were not a Martian."

"The Martian race has never had the slightest tendency toward homicide. A Martian Regenerator doesn't even process the concept. Of course the Regenerator will treat him. It has to. But what will it treat?"

"Oh," said Haskins.

"That poor devil must be stopped before—you say he was homicidal? I don't know what will happen! Quick, what is his address?"

"Well, Mr. Follansby, he was in such a terrible hurry—"

The manager gave him a long, unbelieving look. "Get the police! Call the General Motors Security Division! Find him!"

Haskins raced for the door.

"Wait!" yelled the manager, struggling into a raincoat. "I'm coming, too."

Elwood Caswell returned to his apartment by taxicopter. He lugged the Regenerator into his living room, put it down near the couch and studied it thoughtfully.

"That clerk was right," he said after a while. "It does go with the room."

Esthetically, the Regenerator was a success.

Caswell admired it for a few more moments, then went into the kitchen and fixed himself a chicken sandwich. He ate slowly, staring fixedly at a point just above and to the left of his kitchen clock.

Damn you, Magnessen! Dirty no-good lying shifty-eyed enemy of all that's decent and clean in the world....

Taking the revolver from his pocket, he laid it on the table. With a stiffened forefinger, he poked it into different positions.

It was time to begin therapy.

Except that....

Caswell realized worriedly that he didn't want to lose the desire to kill Magnessen. What would become of him if he lost that urge? His life would lose all purpose, all coherence, all flavor and zest. It would be quite dull, really.

Moreover, he had a great and genuine grievance against Magnessen, one he didn't like to think about.

Irene!

His poor sister, debauched by the subtle and insidious Magnessen, ruined by him and cast aside. What better reason could a man have to take his revolver and....

Caswell finally remembered that he did not have a sister.

Now was really the time to begin therapy.

He went into the living room and found the operating instructions tucked into a ventilation louver of the machine. He opened them and read:

To Operate All Rex Model Regenerators:

1.Place the Regenerator near a comfortable couch. (A comfortable couch can be purchased as an additional accessory from any General Motors dealer.)

2.Plug in the machine.

3.Affix the adjustable contact-band to the forehead.

And that's all! Your Regenerator will do the rest! There will be no language bar or dialect problem, since the Regenerator communicates by Direct Sense Contact (Patent Pending). All you must do is cooperate.

Try not to feel any embarrassment or shame. Everyone has problems and many are worse than yours! Your Regenerator has no interest in your morals or ethical standards, so don't feel it is 'judging' you. It desires only to aid you in becoming well and happy.

As soon as it has collected and processed enough data, your Regenerator will begin treatment. You make the sessions as short or as long as you like. You are the boss! And of course you can end a session at any time.

That's all there is to it! Simple, isn't it? Now plug in your General Motors Regenerator and GET SANE!

"Nothing hard about that," Caswell said to himself. He pushed the Regenerator closer to the couch and plugged it in. He lifted the headband, started to slip it on, stopped.

"I feel so silly!" he giggled.

Abruptly he closed his mouth and stared pugnaciously at the black-and-chrome machine.

"So you think you can make me sane, huh?"

The Regenerator didn't answer.

"Oh, well, go ahead and try." He slipped the headband over his forehead, crossed his arms on his chest and leaned back.

Nothing happened. Caswell settled himself more comfortably on the couch. He scratched his shoulder and put the headband at a more comfortable angle. Still nothing. His thoughts began to wander.

Magnessen! You noisy, overbearing oaf, you disgusting—

"Good afternoon," a voice murmured in his head. "I am your mechanotherapist."

Caswell twitched guiltily. "Hello. I was just—you know, just sort of—"

"Of course," the machine said soothingly. "Don't we all? I am now scanning the material in your preconscious with the intent of synthesis, diagnosis, prognosis, and treatment. I find...."

"Yes?"

"Just one moment." The Regenerator was silent for several minutes. Then, hesitantly, it said, "This is beyond doubt a most unusual case."

"Really?" Caswell asked, pleased.

"Yes. The coefficients seem—I'm not sure...." The machine's robotic voice grew feeble. The pilot light began to flicker and fade.

"Hey, what's the matter?"

"Confusion," said the machine. "Of course," it went on in a stronger voice, "the unusual nature of the symptoms need not prove entirely baffling to a competent therapeutic machine. A symptom, no matter how bizarre, is no more than a signpost, an indication of inner difficulty. And all symptoms can be related to the broad mainstream of proven theory. Since the theory is effective, the symptoms must relate. We will proceed on that assumption."

"Are you sure you know what you're doing?" asked Caswell, feeling lightheaded.

The machine snapped back, its pilot light blazing. "Mechanotherapy today is an exact science and admits no significant errors. We will proceed with a word-association test."

"Fire away," said Caswell.

"House?"

"Home."

"Dog?"

"Cat."

"Fleefl?"

Caswell hesitated, trying to figure out the word. It sounded vaguely Martian, but it might be Venusian or even—

"Fleefl?" the Regenerator repeated.

"Marfoosh," Caswell replied, making up the word on the spur of the moment.

"Loud?"

"Sweet."

"Green?"

"Mother."

"Thanagoyes?"

"Patamathonga."

"Arrides?"

"Nexothesmodrastica."

"Chtheesnohelgnopteces?"

"Rigamaroo latasentricpropatria!" Caswell shot back. It was a collection of sounds he was particularly proud of. The average man would not have been able to pronounce them.

"Hmm," said the Regenerator. "The pattern fits. It always does."

"What pattern?"

"You have," the machine informed him, "a classic case of feem desire, complicated by strong dwarkish intentions."

"I do? I thought I was homicidal."

"That term has no referent," the machine said severely. "Therefore I must reject it as nonsense syllabification. Now consider these points: The feem desire is perfectly normal. Never forget that. But it is usually replaced at an early age by the hovendish revulsion. Individuals lacking in this basic environmental response—"

"I'm not absolutely sure I know what you're talking about," Caswell confessed.

"Please, sir! We must establish one thing at once. You are the patient. I am the mechanotherapist. You have brought your troubles to me for treatment. But you cannot expect help unless you cooperate."

"All right," Caswell said. "I'll try."

Up to now, he had been bathed in a warm glow of superiority. Everything the machine said had seemed mildly humorous. As a matter of fact, he had felt capable of pointing out a few things wrong with the mechanotherapist.

Now that sense of well-being evaporated, as it always did, and Caswell was alone, terribly alone and lost, a creature of his compulsions, in search of a little peace and contentment.

He would undergo anything to find them. Sternly he reminded himself that he had no right to comment on the mechanotherapist. These machines knew what they were doing and had been doing it for a long time. He would cooperate, no matter how outlandish the treatment seemed from his layman's viewpoint.

But it was obvious, Caswell thought, settling himself grimly on the couch, that mechanotherapy was going to be far more difficult than he had imagined.

The search for the missing customer had been brief and useless. He was nowhere to be found on the teeming New York streets and no one could remember seeing a red-haired, red-eyed little man lugging a black therapeutic machine.

It was all too common a sight.

In answer to an urgent telephone call, the police came immediately, four of them, led by a harassed young lieutenant of detectives named Smith.

Smith just had time to ask, "Say, why don't you people put tags on things?" when there was an interruption.

A man pushed his way past the policeman at the door. He was tall and gnarled and ugly, and his eyes were deep-set and bleakly blue. His clothes, unpressed and uncaring, hung on him like corrugated iron.

"What do you want?" Lieutenant Smith asked.

The ugly man flipped back his lapel, showing a small silver badge beneath. "I'm John Rath, General Motors Security Division."

"Oh ... Sorry, sir," Lieutenant Smith said, saluting. "I didn't think you people would move in so fast."

Rath made a noncommittal noise. "Have you checked for prints, Lieutenant? The customer might have touched some other therapy machine."

"I'll get right on it, sir," Smith said. It wasn't often that one of the operatives from GM, GE, or IBM came down to take a personal hand. If a local cop showed he was really clicking, there just might be the possibility of an Industrial Transfer....

Rath turned to Follansby and Haskins, and transfixed them with a gaze as piercing and as impersonal as a radar beam. "Let's have the full story," he said, taking a notebook and pencil from a shapeless pocket.

He listened to the tale in ominous silence. Finally he closed his notebook, thrust it back into his pocket and said, "The therapeutic machines are a sacred trust. To give a customer the wrong machine is a betrayal of that trust, a violation of the Public Interest, and a defamation of the Company's good reputation."

The manager nodded in agreement, glaring at his unhappy clerk.

"A Martian model," Rath continued, "should never have been on the floor in the first place."

"I can explain that," Follansby said hastily. "We needed a demonstrator model and I wrote to the Company, telling them—"

"This might," Rath broke in inexorably, "be considered a case of gross criminal negligence."

Both the manager and the clerk exchanged horrified looks. They were thinking of the General Motors Reformatory outside of Detroit, where Company offenders passed their days in sullen silence, monotonously drawing microcircuits for pocket television sets.

"However, that is out of my jurisdiction," Rath said. He turned his baleful gaze full upon Haskins. "You are certain that the customer never mentioned his name?"

"No, sir. I mean yes, I'm sure," Haskins replied rattledly.

"Did he mention any names at all?"

Haskins plunged his face into his hands. He looked up and said eagerly, "Yes! He wanted to kill someone! A friend of his!"

"Who?" Rath asked, with terrible patience.

"The friend's name was—let me think—Magneton! That was it! Magneton! Or was it Morrison? Oh, dear...."

Mr. Rath's iron face registered a rather corrugated disgust. People were useless as witnesses. Worse than useless, since they were frequently misleading. For reliability, give him a robot every time.

"Didn't he mention anything significant?"

"Let me think!" Haskins said, his face twisting into a fit of concentration.

Rath waited.

Mr. Follansby cleared his throat. "I was just thinking, Mr. Rath. About that Martian machine. It won't treat a Terran homicidal case as homicidal, will it?"

"Of course not. Homicide is unknown on Mars."

"Yes. But what will it do? Might it not reject the entire case as unsuitable? Then the customer would merely return the Regenerator with a complaint and we would—"

Mr. Rath shook his head. "The Rex Regenerator must treat if it finds evidence of psychosis. By Martian standards, the customer is a very sick man, a psychotic—no matter what is wrong with him."

Follansby removed his pince-nez and polished them rapidly. "What will the machine do, then?"

"It will treat him for the Martian illness most analogous to his case. Feem desire, I should imagine, with various complications. As for what will happen once treatment begins, I don't know. I doubt whether anyone knows, since it has never happened before. Offhand, I would say there are two major alternatives: the patient may reject the therapy out of hand, in which case he is left with his homicidal mania unabated. Or he may accept the Martian therapy and reach a cure."

Mr. Follansby's face brightened. "Ah! A cure is possible!"

"You don't understand," Rath said. "He may effect a cure of his nonexistent Martian psychosis. But to cure something that is not there is, in effect, to erect a gratuitous delusional system. You might say that the machine would work in reverse, producing psychosis instead of removing it."

Mr. Follansby groaned and leaned against a Bell Psychosomatica.

"The result," Rath summed up, "would be to convince the customer that he was a Martian. A sane Martian, naturally."

Haskins suddenly shouted, "I remember! I remember now! He said he worked for the New York Rapid Transit Corporation! I remember distinctly!"

"That's a break," Rath said, reaching for the telephone.

Haskins wiped his perspiring face in relief. "And I just remembered something else that should make it easier still."

"What?"

"The customer said he had been an alcoholic at one time. I'm sure of it, because he was interested at first in the IBM Alcoholic Reliever, until I talked him out of it. He had red hair, you know, and I've had a theory for some time about red-headedness and alcoholism. It seems—"

"Excellent," Rath said. "Alcoholism will be on his records. It narrows the search considerably."

As he dialed the NYRT Corporation, the expression on his craglike face was almost pleasant.

It was good, for a change, to find that a human could retain some significant facts.

"But surely you remember your goricae?" the Regenerator was saying.

"No," Caswell answered wearily.

"Tell me, then, about your juvenile experiences with the thorastrian fleep."

"Never had any."

"Hmm. Blockage," muttered the machine. "Resentment. Repression. Are you sure you don't remember your goricae and what it meant to you? The experience is universal."

"Not for me," Caswell said, swallowing a yawn.

He had been undergoing mechanotherapy for close to four hours and it struck him as futile. For a while, he had talked voluntarily about his childhood, his mother and father, his older brother. But the Regenerator had asked him to put aside those fantasies. The patient's relationships to an imaginary parent or sibling, it explained, were unworkable and of minor importance psychologically. The important thing was the patient's feelings—both revealed and repressed—toward his goricae.

"Aw, look," Caswell complained, "I don't even know what a goricae is."

"Of course you do. You just won't let yourself know."

"I don't know. Tell me."

"It would be better if you told me."

"How can I?" Caswell raged. "I don't know!"

"What do you imagine a goricae would be?"

"A forest fire," Caswell said. "A salt tablet. A jar of denatured alcohol. A small screwdriver. Am I getting warm? A notebook. A revolver—"

"These associations are meaningful," the Regenerator assured him. "Your attempt at randomness shows a clearly underlying pattern. Do you begin to recognize it?"

"What in hell is a goricae?" Caswell roared.

"The tree that nourished you during infancy, and well into puberty, if my theory about you is correct. Inadvertently, the goricae stifled your necessary rejection of the feem desire. This in turn gave rise to your present urge to dwark someone in a vlendish manner."

"No tree nourished me."

"You cannot recall the experience?"

"Of course not. It never happened."

"You are sure of that?"

"Positive."

"Not even the tiniest bit of doubt?"

"No! No goricae ever nourished me. Look, I can break off these sessions at any time, right?"

"Of course," the Regenerator said. "But it would not be advisable at this moment. You are expressing anger, resentment, fear. By your rigidly summary rejection—"

"Nuts," said Caswell, and pulled off the headband.

The silence was wonderful. Caswell stood up, yawned, stretched and massaged the back of his neck. He stood in front of the humming black machine and gave it a long leer.

"You couldn't cure me of a common cold," he told it.

Stiffly he walked the length of the living room and returned to the Regenerator.

"Lousy fake!" he shouted.

Caswell went into the kitchen and opened a bottle of beer. His revolver was still on the table, gleaming dully.

Magnessen! You unspeakable treacherous filth! You fiend incarnate! You inhuman, hideous monster! Someone must destroy you, Magnessen! Someone....

Someone? He himself would have to do it. Only he knew the bottomless depths of Magnessen's depravity, his viciousness, his disgusting lust for power.

Yes, it was his duty, Caswell thought. But strangely, the knowledge brought him no pleasure.

After all, Magnessen was his friend.

He stood up, ready for action. He tucked the revolver into his right-hand coat pocket and glanced at the kitchen clock. Nearly six-thirty. Magnessen would be home now, gulping his dinner, grinning over his plans.

This was the perfect time to take him.

Caswell strode to the door, opened it, started through, and stopped.

A thought had crossed his mind, a thought so tremendously involved, so meaningful, so far-reaching in its implications that he was stirred to his depths. Caswell tried desperately to shake off the knowledge it brought. But the thought, permanently etched upon his memory, would not depart.

Under the circumstances, he could do only one thing.

He returned to the living room, sat down on the couch and slipped on the headband.

The Regenerator said, "Yes?"

"It's the damnedest thing," Caswell said, "but do you know, I think I do remember my goricae!"

John Rath contacted the New York Rapid Transit Corporation by televideo and was put into immediate contact with Mr. Bemis, a plump, tanned man with watchful eyes.

"Alcoholism?" Mr. Bemis repeated, after the problem was explained. Unobtrusively, he turned on his tape recorder. "Among our employees?" Pressing a button beneath his foot, Bemis alerted Transit Security, Publicity, Intercompany Relations, and the Psychoanalysis Division. This done, he looked earnestly at Rath. "Not a chance of it, my dear sir. Just between us, why does General Motors really want to know?"

Rath smiled bitterly. He should have anticipated this. NYRT and GM had had their differences in the past. Officially, there was cooperation between the two giant corporations. But for all practical purposes—

"The question is in terms of the Public Interest," Rath said.

"Oh, certainly," Mr. Bemis replied, with a subtle smile. Glancing at his tattle board, he noticed that several company executives had tapped in on his line. This might mean a promotion, if handled properly.

"The Public Interest of GM," Mr. Bemis added with polite nastiness. "The insinuation is, I suppose, that drunken conductors are operating our jetbuses and helis?"

"Of course not. I was searching for a single alcoholic predilection, an individual latency—"

"There's no possibility of it. We at Rapid Transit do not hire people with even the merest tendency in that direction. And may I suggest, sir, that you clean your own house before making implications about others?"

And with that, Mr. Bemis broke the connection.

No one was going to put anything over on him.

"Dead end," Rath said heavily. He turned and shouted, "Smith! Did you find any prints?"

Lieutenant Smith, his coat off and sleeves rolled up, bounded over. "Nothing usable, sir."

Rath's thin lips tightened. It had been close to seven hours since the customer had taken the Martian machine. There was no telling what harm had been done by now. The customer would be justified in bringing suit against the Company. Not that the money mattered much; it was the bad publicity that was to be avoided at all costs.

"Beg pardon, sir," Haskins said.

Rath ignored him. What next? Rapid Transit was not going to cooperate. Would the Armed Services make their records available for scansion by somatotype and pigmentation?

"Sir," Haskins said again.

"What is it?"

"I just remembered the customer's friend's name. It was Magnessen."

"Are you sure of that?"

"Absolutely," Haskins said, with the first confidence he had shown in hours. "I've taken the liberty of looking him up in the telephone book, sir. There's only one Manhattan listing under that name."

Rath glowered at him from under shaggy eyebrows. "Haskins, I hope you are not wrong about this. I sincerely hope that."

"I do too, sir," Haskins admitted, feeling his knees begin to shake.

"Because if you are," Rath said, "I will ... Never mind. Let's go!"

By police escort, they arrived at the address in fifteen minutes. It was an ancient brownstone and Magnessen's name was on a second-floor door. They knocked.

The door opened and a stocky, crop-headed, shirt-sleeved man in his thirties stood before them. He turned slightly pale at the sight of so many uniforms, but held his ground.

"What is this?" he demanded.

"You Magnessen?" Lieutenant Smith barked.

"Yeah. What's the beef? If it's about my hi-fi playing too loud, I can tell you that old hag downstairs—"

"May we come in?" Rath asked. "It's important."

Magnessen seemed about to refuse, so Rath pushed past him, followed by Smith, Follansby, Haskins, and a small army of policemen. Magnessen turned to face them, bewildered, defiant and more than a little awed.

"Mr. Magnessen," Rath said, in the pleasantest voice he could muster, "I hope you'll forgive the intrusion. Let me assure you, it is in the Public Interest, as well as your own. Do you know a short, angry-looking, red-haired, red-eyed man?"

"Yes," Magnessen said slowly and warily.

Haskins let out a sigh of relief.

"Would you tell us his name and address?" asked Rath.

"I suppose you mean—hold it! What's he done?"

"Nothing."

"Then what you want him for?"

"There's no time for explanations," Rath said. "Believe me, it's in his own best interest, too. What is his name?"

Magnessen studied Rath's ugly, honest face, trying to make up his mind.

Lieutenant Smith said, "Come on, talk, Magnessen, if you know what's good for you. We want the name and we want it quick."

It was the wrong approach. Magnessen lighted a cigarette, blew smoke in Smith's direction and inquired, "You got a warrant, buddy?"

"You bet I have," Smith said, striding forward. "I'll warrant you, wise guy."

"Stop it!" Rath ordered. "Lieutenant Smith, thank you for your assistance. I won't need you any longer."

Smith left sulkily, taking his platoon with him.

Rath said, "I apologize for Smith's over-eagerness. You had better hear the problem." Briefly but fully, he told the story of the customer and the Martian therapeutic machine.

When he was finished, Magnessen looked more suspicious than ever. "You say he wants to kill me?"

"Definitely."

"That's a lie! I don't know what your game is, mister, but you'll never make me believe that. Elwood's my best friend. We been best friends since we was kids. We been in service together. Elwood would cut off his arm for me. And I'd do the same for him."

"Yes, yes," Rath said impatiently, "in a sane frame of mind, he would. But your friend Elwood—is that his first name or last?"

"First," Magnessen said tauntingly.

"Your friend Elwood is psychotic."

"You don't know him. That guy loves me like a brother. Look, what's Elwood really done? Defaulted on some payments or something? I can help out."

"You thickheaded imbecile!" Rath shouted. "I'm trying to save your life, and the life and sanity of your friend!"

"But how do I know?" Magnessen pleaded. "You guys come busting in here—"

"You can trust me," Rath said.

Magnessen studied Rath's face and nodded sourly. "His name's Elwood Caswell. He lives just down the block at number 341."

The man who came to the door was short, with red hair and red-rimmed eyes. His right hand was thrust into his coat pocket. He seemed very calm.

"Are you Elwood Caswell?" Rath asked. "The Elwood Caswell who bought a Regenerator early this afternoon at the Home Therapy Appliances Store?"

"Yes," said Caswell. "Won't you come in?"

Inside Caswell's small living room, they saw the Regenerator, glistening black and chrome, standing near the couch. It was unplugged.

"Have you used it?" Rath asked anxiously.

"Yes."

Follansby stepped forward. "Mr. Caswell, I don't know how to explain this, but we made a terrible mistake. The Regenerator you took was a Martian model—for giving therapy to Martians."

"I know," said Caswell.

"You do?"

"Of course. It became pretty obvious after a while."

"It was a dangerous situation," Rath said. "Especially for a man with your—ah—troubles." He studied Caswell covertly. The man seemed fine, but appearances were frequently deceiving, especially with psychotics. Caswell had been homicidal; there was no reason why he should not still be.

And Rath began to wish he had not dismissed Smith and his policemen so summarily. Sometimes an armed squad was a comforting thing to have around.

Caswell walked across the room to the therapeutic machine. One hand was still in his jacket pocket; the other he laid affectionately upon the Regenerator.

"The poor thing tried its best," he said. "Of course, it couldn't cure what wasn't there." He laughed. "But it came very near succeeding!"

Rath studied Caswell's face and said, in a trained, casual tone, "Glad there was no harm, sir. The Company will, of course, reimburse you for your lost time and for your mental anguish—"

"Naturally," Caswell said.

"—and we will substitute a proper Terran Regenerator at once."

"That won't be necessary."

"It won't?"

"No." Caswell's voice was decisive. "The machine's attempt at therapy forced me into a compete self-appraisal. There was a moment of absolute insight, during which I was able to evaluate and discard my homicidal intentions toward poor Magnessen."

Rath nodded dubiously. "You feel no such urge now?"

"Not in the slightest."

Rath frowned deeply, started to say something, and stopped. He turned to Follansby and Haskins. "Get that machine out of here. I'll have a few things to say to you at the store."

The manager and the clerk lifted the Regenerator and left.

Rath took a deep breath. "Mr. Caswell, I would strongly advise that you accept a new Regenerator from the Company, gratis. Unless a cure is effected in a proper mechanotherapeutic manner, there is always the danger of a setback."

"No danger with me," Caswell said, airily but with deep conviction. "Thank you for your consideration, sir. And good night."

Rath shrugged and walked to the door.

"Wait!" Caswell called.

Rath turned. Caswell had taken his hand out of his pocket. In it was a revolver. Rath felt sweat trickle down his arms. He calculated the distance between himself and Caswell. Too far.

"Here," Caswell said, extending the revolver butt-first. "I won't need this any longer."

Rath managed to keep his face expressionless as he accepted the revolver and stuck it into a shapeless pocket.

"Good night," Caswell said. He closed the door behind Rath and bolted it.

At last he was alone.

Caswell walked into the kitchen. He opened a bottle of beer, took a deep swallow and sat down at the kitchen table. He stared fixedly at a point just above and to the left of the clock.

He had to form his plans now. There was no time to lose.

Magnessen! That inhuman monster who cut down the Caswell goricae! Magnessen! The man who, even now, was secretly planning to infect New York with the abhorrent feem desire! Oh, Magnessen, I wish you a long, long life, filled with the torture I can inflict on you. And to start with....

Caswell smiled to himself as he planned exactly how he would dwark Magnessen in a vlendish manner.

2BR02B

by Kurt Vonnegut, Jr.

Everything was perfectly swell.

There were no prisons, no slums, no insane asylums, no cripples, no poverty, no wars.

All diseases were conquered. So was old age.

Death, barring accidents, was an adventure for volunteers.

The population of the United States was stabilized at forty-million souls.

One bright morning in the Chicago Lying-in Hospital, a man named Edward K. Wehling, Jr., waited for his wife to give birth. He was the only man waiting. Not many people were born a day any more.

Wehling was fifty-six, a mere stripling in a population whose average age was one hundred and twenty-nine.

X-rays had revealed that his wife was going to have triplets. The children would be his first.

Young Wehling was hunched in his chair, his head in his hand. He was so rumpled, so still and colorless as to be virtually invisible. His camouflage was perfect, since the waiting room had a disorderly and demoralized air, too. Chairs and ashtrays had been moved away from the walls. The floor was paved with spattered dropcloths.

The room was being redecorated. It was being redecorated as a memorial to a man who had volunteered to die.

A sardonic old man, about two hundred years old, sat on a stepladder, painting a mural he did not like. Back in the days when people aged visibly, his age would have been guessed at thirty-five or so. Aging had touched him that much before the cure for aging was found.

The mural he was working on depicted a very neat garden. Men and women in white, doctors and nurses, turned the soil, planted seedlings, sprayed bugs, spread fertilizer.

Men and women in purple uniforms pulled up weeds, cut down plants that were old and sickly, raked leaves, carried refuse to trash-burners.

Never, never, never—not even in medieval Holland nor old Japan—had a garden been more formal, been better tended. Every plant had all the loam, light, water, air and nourishment it could use.

A hospital orderly came down the corridor, singing under his breath a popular song:

If you don't like my kisses, honey,
Here's what I will do:
I'll go see a girl in purple,
Kiss this sad world toodle-oo.
If you don't want my lovin',
Why should I take up all this space?
I'll get off this old planet,
Let some sweet baby have my place.

The orderly looked in at the mural and the muralist. "Looks so real," he said, "I can practically imagine I'm standing in the middle of it."

"What makes you think you're not in it?" said the painter. He gave a satiric smile. "It's called 'The Happy Garden of Life,' you know."

"That's good of Dr. Hitz," said the orderly.

He was referring to one of the male figures in white, whose head was a portrait of Dr. Benjamin Hitz, the hospital's Chief Obstetrician. Hitz was a blindingly handsome man.

"Lot of faces still to fill in," said the orderly. He meant that the faces of many of the figures in the mural were still blank. All blanks were to be filled with portraits of important people on either the hospital staff or from the Chicago Office of the Federal Bureau of Termination.

"Must be nice to be able to make pictures that look like something," said the orderly.

The painter's face curdled with scorn. "You think I'm proud of this daub?" he said. "You think this is my idea of what life really looks like?"

"What's your idea of what life looks like?" said the orderly.

The painter gestured at a foul dropcloth. "There's a good picture of it," he said. "Frame that, and you'll have a picture a damn sight more honest than this one."

"You're a gloomy old duck, aren't you?" said the orderly.

"Is that a crime?" said the painter.

The orderly shrugged. "If you don't like it here, Grandpa—" he said, and he finished the thought with the trick telephone number that people who didn't want to live any more were supposed to call. The zero in the telephone number he pronounced "naught."

The number was: "2 B R 0 2 B."

It was the telephone number of an institution whose fanciful sobriquets included: "Automat," "Birdland," "Cannery," "Catbox," "De-louser," "Easy-go," "Good-by, Mother," "Happy Hooligan," "Kiss-me-quick," "Lucky Pierre," "Sheepdip," "Waring Blendor," "Weep-no-more" and "Why Worry?"

"To be or not to be" was the telephone number of the municipal gas chambers of the Federal Bureau of Termination.

The painter thumbed his nose at the orderly. "When I decide it's time to go," he said, "it won't be at the Sheepdip."

"A do-it-yourselfer, eh?" said the orderly. "Messy business, Grandpa. Why don't you have a little consideration for the people who have to clean up after you?"

The painter expressed with an obscenity his lack of concern for the tribulations of his survivors. "The world could do with a good deal more mess, if you ask me," he said.

The orderly laughed and moved on.

Wehling, the waiting father, mumbled something without raising his head. And then he fell silent again.

A coarse, formidable woman strode into the waiting room on spike heels. Her shoes, stockings, trench coat, bag and overseas cap were all purple, the purple the painter called "the color of grapes on Judgment Day."

The medallion on her purple musette bag was the seal of the Service Division of the Federal Bureau of Termination, an eagle perched on a turnstile.

The woman had a lot of facial hair—an unmistakable mustache, in fact. A curious thing about gas-chamber hostesses was that, no matter how lovely and feminine they were when recruited, they all sprouted mustaches within five years or so.

"Is this where I'm supposed to come?" she said to the painter.

"A lot would depend on what your business was," he said. "You aren't about to have a baby, are you?"

"They told me I was supposed to pose for some picture," she said. "My name's Leora Duncan." She waited.

"And you dunk people," he said.

"What?" she said.

"Skip it," he said.

"That sure is a beautiful picture," she said. "Looks just like heaven or something."

"Or something," said the painter. He took a list of names from his smock pocket. "Duncan, Duncan, Duncan," he said, scanning the list. "Yes—here you are. You're entitled to be immortalized. See any faceless body here you'd like me to stick your head on? We've got a few choice ones left."

She studied the mural bleakly. "Gee," she said, "they're all the same to me. I don't know anything about art."

"A body's a body, eh?" he said, "All righty. As a master of fine art, I recommend this body here." He indicated a faceless figure of a woman who was carrying dried stalks to a trash-burner.

"Well," said Leora Duncan, "that's more the disposal people, isn't it? I mean, I'm in service. I don't do any disposing."

The painter clapped his hands in mock delight. "You say you don't know anything about art, and then you prove in the next breath that you know more about it than I do! Of course the sheave-carrier is wrong for a hostess! A snipper, a pruner—that's more your line." He pointed to a figure in purple who was sawing a dead branch from an apple tree. "How about her?" he said. "You like her at all?"

"Gosh—" she said, and she blushed and became humble—"that—that puts me right next to Dr. Hitz."

"That upsets you?" he said.

"Good gravy, no!" she said. "It's—it's just such an honor."

"Ah, You admire him, eh?" he said.

"Who doesn't admire him?" she said, worshiping the portrait of Hitz. It was the portrait of a tanned, white-haired, omnipotent Zeus, two hundred and forty years old. "Who doesn't admire him?" she said again. "He was responsible for setting up the very first gas chamber in Chicago."

"Nothing would please me more," said the painter, "than to put you next to him for all time. Sawing off a limb—that strikes you as appropriate?"

"That is kind of like what I do," she said. She was demure about what she did. What she did was make people comfortable while she killed them.

And, while Leora Duncan was posing for her portrait, into the waitingroom bounded Dr. Hitz himself. He was seven feet tall, and he boomed with importance, accomplishments, and the joy of living.

"Well, Miss Duncan! Miss Duncan!" he said, and he made a joke. "What are you doing here?" he said. "This isn't where the people leave. This is where they come in!"

"We're going to be in the same picture together," she said shyly.

"Good!" said Dr. Hitz heartily. "And, say, isn't that some picture?"

"I sure am honored to be in it with you," she said.

"Let me tell you," he said, "I'm honored to be in it with you. Without women like you, this wonderful world we've got wouldn't be possible."

He saluted her and moved toward the door that led to the delivery rooms. "Guess what was just born," he said.

"I can't," she said.

"Triplets!" he said.

"Triplets!" she said. She was exclaiming over the legal implications of triplets.

The law said that no newborn child could survive unless the parents of the child could find someone who would volunteer to die. Triplets, if they were all to live, called for three volunteers.

"Do the parents have three volunteers?" said Leora Duncan.

"Last I heard," said Dr. Hitz, "they had one, and were trying to scrape another two up."

"I don't think they made it," she said. "Nobody made three appointments with us. Nothing but singles going through today, unless somebody called in after I left. What's the name?"

"Wehling," said the waiting father, sitting up, red-eyed and frowzy. "Edward K. Wehling, Jr., is the name of the happy father-to-be."

He raised his right hand, looked at a spot on the wall, gave a hoarsely wretched chuckle. "Present," he said.

"Oh, Mr. Wehling," said Dr. Hitz, "I didn't see you."

"The invisible man," said Wehling.

"They just phoned me that your triplets have been born," said Dr. Hitz. "They're all fine, and so is the mother. I'm on my way in to see them now."

"Hooray," said Wehling emptily.

"You don't sound very happy," said Dr. Hitz.

"What man in my shoes wouldn't be happy?" said Wehling. He gestured with his hands to symbolize care-free simplicity. "All I have to do is pick out which one of the triplets is going to live, then deliver my maternal grandfather to the Happy Hooligan, and come back here with a receipt."

Dr. Hitz became rather severe with Wehling, towered over him. "You don't believe in population control, Mr. Wehling?" he said.

"I think it's perfectly keen," said Wehling tautly.

"Would you like to go back to the good old days, when the population of the Earth was twenty billion—about to become forty billion, then eighty billion, then one hundred and sixty billion? Do you know what a drupelet is, Mr. Wehling?" said Hitz.

"Nope," said Wehling sulkily.

"A drupelet, Mr. Wehling, is one of the little knobs, one of the little pulpy grains of a blackberry," said Dr. Hitz. "Without population control, human beings would now be packed on this surface of this old planet like drupelets on a blackberry! Think of it!"

Wehling continued to stare at the same spot on the wall.

"In the year 2000," said Dr. Hitz, "before scientists stepped in and laid down the law, there wasn't even enough drinking water to go around, and nothing to eat but sea-weed—and still people insisted on their right to reproduce like jackrabbits. And their right, if possible, to live forever."

"I want those kids," said Wehling quietly. "I want all three of them."

"Of course you do," said Dr. Hitz. "That's only human."

"I don't want my grandfather to die, either," said Wehling.

"Nobody's really happy about taking a close relative to the Catbox," said Dr. Hitz gently, sympathetically.

"I wish people wouldn't call it that," said Leora Duncan.

"What?" said Dr. Hitz.

"I wish people wouldn't call it 'the Catbox,' and things like that," she said. "It gives people the wrong impression."

"You're absolutely right," said Dr. Hitz. "Forgive me." He corrected himself, gave the municipal gas chambers their official title, a title no one ever used in conversation. "I should have said, 'Ethical Suicide Studios,'" he said.

"That sounds so much better," said Leora Duncan.

"This child of yours—whichever one you decide to keep, Mr. Wehling," said Dr. Hitz. "He or she is going to live on a happy, roomy, clean, rich planet, thanks to population control. In a garden like that mural there." He shook his head. "Two centuries ago, when I was a young man, it was a hell that nobody thought could last another twenty years. Now centuries of peace and plenty stretch before us as far as the imagination cares to travel."

He smiled luminously.

The smile faded as he saw that Wehling had just drawn a revolver.

Wehling shot Dr. Hitz dead. "There's room for one—a great big one," he said.

And then he shot Leora Duncan. "It's only death," he said to her as she fell. "There! Room for two."

And then he shot himself, making room for all three of his children.

Nobody came running. Nobody, seemingly, heard the shots.

The painter sat on the top of his stepladder, looking down reflectively on the sorry scene.

The painter pondered the mournful puzzle of life demanding to be born and, once born, demanding to be fruitful ... to multiply and to live as long as possible—to do all that on a very small planet that would have to last forever.

All the answers that the painter could think of were grim. Even grimmer, surely, than a Catbox, a Happy Hooligan, an Easy Go. He thought of war. He thought of plague. He thought of starvation.

He knew that he would never paint again. He let his paintbrush fall to the drop-cloths below. And then he decided he had had about enough of life in the Happy Garden of Life, too, and he came slowly down from the ladder.

He took Wehling's pistol, really intending to shoot himself.

But he didn't have the nerve.

And then he saw the telephone booth in the corner of the room. He went to it, dialed the well-remembered number: "2 B R O 2 B."

"Federal Bureau of Termination," said the very warm voice of a hostess.

"How soon could I get an appointment?" he asked, speaking very carefully.

"We could probably fit you in late this afternoon, sir," she said. "It might even be earlier, if we get a cancellation."

"All right," said the painter, "fit me in, if you please." And he gave her his name, spelling it out.

"Thank you, sir," said the hostess. "Your city thanks you; your country thanks you; your planet thanks you. But the deepest thanks of all is from future generations."

The Cyber Way
By Jamie Wild

Shea broke the interface with the computer and looked up at his two employers. "You're all set. Now, about my fee."

"Yes, about your fee . . ."

The fuckers were going to stiff him, Shea could see it in their eyes. He took a step forward; if things got nasty he needed to be close enough for his enhanced nervous system's speed to be a factor. "Look, guys, I delivered as promised. You're going to make millions of units out of this. Don't get greedy, it's not worth it. Think about it, you only owe me twenty thousand units. If you stiff me you'll never get another cyborg to work for you, and that's suicide in your line of business."

Morton smiled. "*If* anyone finds out that we stiffed you."

"I'm sure as hell not going to be quiet about it," Shea said with more than just a little heat.

"That's what we figured," Morton's partner Trask said, reaching into his suit jacket.

Shea stepped forward and slammed his hand, fingers forward, into the son-of-a-bitch's chest. Shea's finger bones had been replaced with titanium steel, so he had no trouble smashing through the moron's rib cage, crushing his heart. Shea watched the look of astonishment on Trask's face. It was funny, they always looked so damn surprised, stupid shits. Shea let the body fall to the floor and then he reached into the suit jacket. He came away with a military battle pistol. This guy had been serious heat; he was no partner. Shea turned back to Morton and pointed the weapon at him. "Now, about my fee?"

"Jesus Christ, Jesus Christ. . ."

"I don't give a shit about your god, I just want my money."

"Please, please don't kill me."

"Twenty thousand units."

"I haven't got it."

Shea shook his head. Fucking lightweight. "What do you have?"

"I've got five with me, but I can get you the rest."

Yeah right, Shea thought. "I'm not sure why I'm going to tell you this, since it won't do you any good, but I am. When you play with the big boys, you either need to be honest or you need to be very good, and, friend, you're neither." Shea pulled the trigger and watched as red splotches erupted on Morton's chest. It took him three minutes to find the five thousand units and then let himself out of the hotel room.

This was not good, he'd been counting on that money. He wished to hell he could use the little banking scam that he had just set up for Morton, but he couldn't. You had to work at the bank to be able to use that little scam, and Shea was never going to work that side of the street. No, he didn't need that. But still, his next payment was due and he was now ten thousand units short. Hell, he didn't even have the money to make the rent. Even so, he was doing better than most cyborgs: after five years he was still a free agent. By this time, most cyborgs had fallen behind on their payments and had indentured themselves to The Consortium. That was not for Shea. The jobs were dangerous and the pay was for shit. It wasn't supposed to be like this. It was supposed to be glamorous, he was supposed to rich, people he didn't even know were supposed to love him. Damn, damn, damn!

His cellular phone began to ring.

Shea reached into his leather duster and took out the phone. "Shea here," he said, hoping that the call didn't have anything to do with the death of his former employer.

"Mr. Shea, this is Shelly and I'm calling for Mr. McCormick. He has some work for you. How soon can you be here?"

Shea smiled. "I'll be there in ten minutes."

"Very good." The connection broke.

This was indeed good. McCormick's work was usually dull, but it paid well and McCormick was dependable. Shea might make it one more month without becoming indentured. Maybe.

Ten minutes later Shea was in McCormick's office waiting for him. The office was spacious and tastefully decorated. Deeply polished mahoganies dominated the room. Five minutes later McCormick and another man arrived. The two looked to be of a kind, clean shaven, military hair cuts, and even though they were both in street clothes it was clear that they would be more comfortable in uniforms. These weren't guys that you wanted to cross.

"Thanks for getting here on such short notice. I've got an interesting project for you. It should be much more challenging than your usual fare."

Shea brightened. This is what I need. "Great, what do you have in mind?"

"Shea, this is Tom Anderson. He's one of my closest friends. I'm sure you've heard me talk about him. Someone's trying to kill him. We need you to help us find out who that someone is. I'm willing to give you double your normal fee."

Thank God! "Sounds good," Shea said to McCormick. Of Anderson he asked, "How do you know that someone is trying to kill you?"

"There's been an attempt on my life on each of the last two planets I've been to. I captured the first assassin. He told me that he was a member of The Consortium and that I was fair game. The second assassin was a cyborg, I had one hell of a time killing him."

Shea took another look at Anderson. Real men weren't supposed to be that dangerous. This guy should only exist in a holo-vision program. "Jesus Christ, what do you need my help for?"

"I want to stop the attempts on my life. If you find out who's offering the contract, then I can find the responsible party and convince them to cancel it."

God, I hope I'm not getting in over my head. "Okay. Where did the attacks happen?"

"The first one was on Eden, the second was on Tristan."

"You killed the man on Tristan?"

"I killed a *cyborg* on Tristan."

Just what I fucking need, a killer with an attitude. "Well, Eden's too far away for me to find anything out via the computer. But Tristan's within my range. Mind if I interface with your computer, McCormick?"

"Please do."

Shea took a small clear unit from his jacket and plugged it into McCormick's mobile computer. He saw Anderson go white. The man was visibly shaken and clenching his chair for all he was worth. Fucking mundane. As the interface completed Shea felt the flow of the matrix envelop him. The temptation to let himself be swallowed up in the energy current was a strong one. No matter how frequently he moved along the net, that temptation never weakened. He focused his awareness on the grid that spread out before him. McCormick's system was a good one; it dumped Shea several layers below where most systems would have. He was able to avoid a lot of the menial hacking that one normally had to do to get to the more interesting parts of the net. Shea found the energy flow that would lead him to the news reports on Tristan and followed it. Once there, the raw data flooded his senses. He let it wash through his mind and then he picked out the meaningful parts.

According to the report, Lem Detrick had been the assailant. Two police officers had died, and in a bizarre accident Detrick had been hit by a subway train.

Looking for more helpful information, Shea moved along the net until he found a way into Tristan's police records. He circumnavigated three levels of security almost effortlessly and immersed himself in the police report. Officers Burke and Tereshko had been killed. Burke had definitely been killed by the cyborg, but it was unclear who had killed Tereshko. An unidentified male had been seen running from the scene, but it was unknown if that man had been involved with the killings. Further, Tereshko's vehicle had turned up in a subway station outside of the port. The unidentified man was being sought for questioning. At the moment they had no leads as to his whereabouts or his identity. Shea backed out, leaving no trail, and exited the matrix. He'd been there less than a minute.

He looked at Anderson. "Do you have any idea who that cyborg you killed was?"

"None."

"You killed Lem Detrick."

"So?"

"So, he's probably the best hit man in the sector. I mean he was. He had this thing about killing at close range. I guess that's what did him in. How did you get him?"

"In the end, I didn't. He got hit by a train, but if I had been holding more than a nine millimeter when I outdrew him, I would have killed him. As it was, I only knocked him down."

Outdrew him? Jesus Christ, what was this guy? "You couldn't have outdrawn him. His nervous system was cybernetically enhanced. He had to be at least twice as fast as you."

"Maybe he missed his last tuneup."

"Jack, I thought all those stories you told me about Anderson The Enforcer were bullshit, but this guy is the genuine article."

"Was I implicated in any of the killings?"

"The report I read mentioned an unidentified male had been spotted running from the scene, but they don't have any leads. It looks like you're in the clear."

"Good, but now how do we find out who hired Detrick?"

"That's a breeze, since Detrick worked for The Consortium, I'll just infiltrate their data banks and rifle their files. Nothing to it."

"Good. When can you start?"

"Is now soon enough?"

McCormick nodded.

Shea interfaced with the computer and was once again immersed in the energy flow. This time he surrendered himself to the flow a bit more than he had the time before. The Consortium was hidden in the matrix several levels below the one he was on. He felt the euphoria of the surging energy as his consciences rushed downwards. It felt very much like riding a white-water raft, only faster. He hit an eddy in the matrix and pulled himself out of the downward flow. This was the level he was looking for. The Consortium's data banks weren't immediately obvious and it took Shea several nanoseconds to locate them and several more to get through nine levels of serious security. The

Consortium's defenses were something. There was stuff here designed to kill. If you didn't know what you were doing, The Consortium would quite happily fry your brain.

Once inside, the information came at Shea in hyper mode. He'd never experienced anything this fast. It was all he could do just to hang onto his identity and let the information wash over him. Much of the data came in the form of incoherent streams, but some of it made sense. The first thing he identified was a blueprint of a Consortium installation. On impulse he sent that to McCormick's printer using a macro that would obscure the path as it went. Then he went searching against the flow for Anderson's name. There it was. He grabbed onto the information in the file and immersed himself in it. A million and a half units had been put down by one Daniel Chen. An immediate solution to the problem presented itself to Shea. All he had to do was switch the names and everything would be fine, for Anderson at least.

As soon as Shea tried to change the data he realized that he had made a terrible mistake. The data could only be changed from a single keyboard and not from cyberspace. Defenses that he hadn't even suspected sprang up all around him and tried to isolate and crush him. For a fraction of a nanosecond he thought they had him, but then he spotted a crack between two of the walls; it was tiny but he got through it and raced away into the matrix. He thought that was the end of it, when a blinding pulse of energy, larger than anything he'd ever seen inside the matrix, exploded from The Consortium's file.

It destroyed everything that it touched as it raced towards him considerably faster than he could every hope to move. Shea ducked down the first level transfer he happened upon. The energy burst followed him, leaving a wake of destruction behind it. Once Shea arrived on the next level, he realized that he was losing ground fast. He caught sight of another downward path. That wouldn't do. The energy burst would catch him before he hit the next level. In desperation he tried a maneuver that he'd only heard about. He went upward in a downward-moving flow. The energy was amazing, and had he not been running for his life he was certain he would have lost his concentration. Then he was out and on the next level. It worked! Shea's relief was short-lived. The energy burst emerged from the flow. He'd gained several nanoseconds, but that was only temporary. Moving for all he was worth, he surveyed the landscape of the matrix for someplace to hide. The sheer destructive force of his pursuer discouraged him from trying any of the host of fancy tricks he knew. He could well imagine himself going through some exotic double-back only to watch the energy pulse smash through the entire thing. He was about to panic when he caught sight of the monolithic data flow that was the Coalition. He'd been here before and knew the way in. The energy burst continued to pursue him, but as soon as it hit the Coalition's flow, serious defenses came up. The resulting fireworks were amazing. At another time Shea would have stuck around and watched the outcome, but at the moment he was more concerned with surviving so he exercised the better part of valor and slunk away.

Shea jumped out of his chair and pulled his interface unit from the computer as if his life depended on it. "Good god, that was close."

"What happened?" McCormick demanded.

"Everything was going fine. I got into their database without too much difficulty. I found out who paid for the contract. Then I decided I could solve everyone's problem by switching Anderson's name with the name of the guy who paid for the hit. When I tried to change the data, all hell broke loose. I've never seen such a powerful defensive setup. It waited until I was completely committed, and then pounced on me. When it wasn't able to crush me, it just came after me, obliterating everything in its path. My god, it'll take the Net Rangers months to repair the damage it caused. I only just managed to divert the power surge that was tracking me to a different computer."

"You do realize that whoever owns the computer you diverted the surge to is going to die, don't you?" Anderson demanded.

"Of course I realize that. I sent the program into the Coalition's data banks. Give me some credit. I'm not going to let innocents get killed. I'm a cyborg, not a monster."

Anderson seemed amused. "They won't mess with the Coalition."

Shea looked at Anderson sharply. "You've got to be joking."

"What do you mean?"

"Everyone knows that The Consortium is sanctioned by the Coalition. In exchange for their cut, they pretend it doesn't exist. The Coalition gets a piece of everyone's pie."

"Not the Coalition that I know."

"Then you're living in a dream, pal."

Anderson started to get up. McCormick put a restraining hand on his shoulder. "We'll talk about it later. Let it go for now."

"Okay then, let's get back to business. Who took the hit out on me?"

Shea went to the print outs. "Here it is, some guy named Chen. A million and a half units; he wants you bad."

"Chen?" Anderson said in apparent astonishment. "He couldn't afford that. He's just the captain of a battleship."

Maybe this guy *was* too stupid to live. "Everyone knows that the commander of a Coalition vessel can make a fortune smuggling. A million and a half units was probably just the money from one trip," Shea said.

Anderson jumped up. "Why you little shit!"

"Tom, calm down," McCormick said sharply, "He's right."

"He's right?"

"Yes, he's right. But that's not important at the moment. What is important is finding a way to get you out of this alive, and make Chen pay."

"I think I've got the answer," Shea said.

"We're listening," McCormick said.

"I had the right idea when I tried to change Anderson's name with Chen's. I just didn't go about it correctly. As I was exiting The Consortium's data banks, I realized that their system is set up so that it can only be altered from a single keyboard. That keyboard is in their main installation."

"How the hell does that help?" Anderson demanded.

"Well, before I went looking for the information you needed, I stumbled onto the floor plans. I figured they might be worth something to someone, so I printed them up. Their physical defenses aren't nearly as impressive as their computer defenses. If you iron men can get me in there, I can change the data. The trick is to get in and out of there without anyone knowing we were there. If The Consortium finds out we broke in, they'll figure out that we changed the database. If that happens, we're in for a world of pain. By the way, I want four times my usual fee." Shea watched the two men, but neither seemed to care about his wage demand. Oh, dear God, let this work out, please let this work out, he thought. This could mean breathing room, he might not have to live from month to month, hell maybe he'd even be able to take some time off.

Anderson looked over the floor plans. "There's no possible way we can get into this place without someone knowing we were there."

"Then you'll just have to hunt this Chen guy down," Shea said, pretending not to care.

Anderson leafed through the plans again. Under them he found an inventory. "According to this inventory, they have five million units, in cash, in their vault. If we broke in and stole it, they might not think to check their data banks. After all, our motive for breaking in would seem clear enough, wouldn't it?"

"You've got a lot of balls," Shea said shaking his head. "Do you have any idea what would happen if The Consortium finds out you stole their money?"

"I'm assuming that they would be very upset with me. Hell, they might even take out a contract on me."

"I see your point, but you can't do it yourself. Anyone who goes in there with you would also be exposed to the danger of retaliation."

"They'd be well paid for the risk. I think that The Consortium has overvalued the fear factor. Fear is not an adequate defense against theft. Not when you're talking about five million units."

"But, if anyone talks, you're dead."

"None of my people would talk," McCormick said. "Do you want in or not?"

"You're going along with this?"

"If Tom thinks we can pull this off, then I'm in."

Oh fuck, Shea thought. This is big. These guys want to take on The Consortium.

"What do you think, Shea? An even share of five million units."

Shea tried not to show his surprise. He hadn't expected them to offer him an equal share. If they could pull this off, he could have anything he'd ever wanted. He'd never have to scrape by again. He couldn't even imagine what that would be like. "How many men would be in on it?"

"You, Jack, myself, and two others should be enough to do the job right. I'm sure you can do the math for yourself."

"A million units. Very tempting." *Of course I'm in, you fucking moron.*

"We need an answer," McCormick said.

"It depends on the other two guys. How trustworthy would they be?"

"I've got five men on the payroll who served with me under Tom. I'm sure any of them would be willing to do whatever it takes to help him out. They'll all be quiet."

"When do you plan to do this?"

"We should be able to come up with a workable plan of action tonight."

"So, you're talking about doing this tomorrow?"

"Tom's up against the gun. We've got to do this as quickly as possible."

Shea smiled. "It's against my better judgment, but count me in."

"Good, meet us here tomorrow, around midnight."

Shea sat back in his rickety easy chair and looked about his dingy efficiency flat. The entire place was three meters square, there were no carpets or rugs over the fiberboard floors, and the walls badly needed a coat of paint. And still, it was a fucking castle compared to what most cyborgs could afford. Shea tried to picture a million units in his checking account. Damn, this was it. The brass ring, everything that he'd ever wanted.

He'd become a cyborg for one reason: money. He wanted lots of it. He wanted to be dirty, rotten, filthy, stinking rich. Nothing more. And these two psycho marines were going to make him just that. No more living in housing projects, existing from one illegal job to the next. Things were going to change. He could see it in his mind's eye. Beautiful women, fast cars, and expensive restaurants. The good life.

He couldn't help but think of the tenements that he'd grown up in. The sound of his neighbors arguing at all hours, the smell of urine in the hallways, and the occasional dead body. When his parents had been killed during a drug deal, he was still only nine years old and he'd had to join a gang to keep on living. There had been no form of welfare on the planet he'd grown up on, not for someone from *his* class. God, that had been a tough way to live. You could never really make enough money to survive, someone from higher up in the gang would always get most of what you brought in. And then he'd found out about The Consortium and the implant, and, worst of all, the financing. At seventeen he really hadn't been able to comprehend how much money he would owe The Consortium, nor how long it would take him to pay it off. But anything was better than the streets. The tenets of his gang, The Stilettos, sounded good: love, honor, and family. Every member of the gang was a member of the family. That was bullshit. They sold you out if they needed to. Took from you whatever they wanted, if they could. The streets had taught him only one thing: no one looked out for you; not ever. You had to cover your own back at all times because you were alone. You were always alone.

To celebrate the job and get a head start on the beginning of his new life Shea had stopped at a trendy store and purchased the most expensive cigar they had, as well as a bottle of their most pretentious champagne, and a copy of *Gourmet Life*. He opened the magazine and began browsing through it. Rather dull, but he'd come to appreciate it. Then he lit the cigar; its foul taste burned down his throat into his lungs. Coughing and sputtering, he reached for a glass of the champagne. The mixture of cigar and champagne was the vilest thing he had ever tasted.

"Shea," Anderson said, "your objective has changed."

"It has?"

"Yes, I don't want you to switch my name with Chen's"

"But, that's the whole point of the mission."

"No, the point of the mission is to stop the attacks on my life. What I want you to do is make it look like I was killed and the contract honored."

"But, then this Chen guy walks."

"No, he doesn't. I'll deal with him personally. I can't let someone else do this for me. That would make me just as bad as Chen."

"So what's wrong with that?"

"A lot. Just do it my way."

"Okay, but I have to do something with the money from the hit."

"Can you just have it deposited into an account without tipping our hand? Then we'll just divvy it up with the rest of the money."

"Yeah, I've got a program that can hide it. I still say it makes more sense to let someone else kill Chen."

"I just can't. Let's go."

McCormick issued everyone a TAZ 12 and combat armor. They brought along three times as much ammo as they intended to use, and enough explosives to level the entire complex if need be. One thing was for sure: these guys weren't lightweights.

Entry wasn't a problem; they flew a heavy flitter through the fence that surrounded the installation. Then they shot their way through glass doors at the main entrance and entered the building. Thirty seconds after they had arrived they were in the control room. The four guards there drew pistols and tried to drive them back. Shea felt sorry for the guards as he watched them get mowed down. They had never had a chance.

McCormick went to the computer and turned the alarm systems off. "There, all's clear on this end."

Anderson took a set of keys from a blood-soaked body and tossed them to Diaz. "One of these keys should fit the computer room door. Escort Shea there. When you're done, make sure these keys find their way back here. We don't want to leave any clues as to why we're *really* here. Then meet us back at the flitter."

Diaz and Shea started off towards the computer room, They found it without any problem and Shea slid into the chair in front of the computer. It took him only a moment to do what was required of him. "We're clear. Let's get the hell out of here."

Diaz nodded, and they started back to the control center to leave the keys. As they entered the room gunfire slammed into them. Diaz went down. Shea raised his rifle and opened fire as he backed out of the room. He never even saw who he was firing at, and he wasn't followed. Once he realized this, Shea turned and ran out of the installation. The others were waiting for him outside.

"Where's Diaz?" Anderson demanded of Shea.

"Diaz bought it when we went back to the control room to return the keys. I was lucky to get out alive."

Anderson looked at McCormick. "We can't leave him there. The Consortium will have us pegged by this time tomorrow."

"You're right. We have to go back."

"Matherson, you and Shea wait here. If things get too hot, you have my permission to leave. We're going back inside."

"You can't go back in there," Shea shouted. "There isn't enough time."

Shea couldn't believe it when Anderson and McCormick ignored him and reentered the building. These guys were out of their fuckin' minds. Cursing, Shea loaded his equipment into the flitter. He could hear sirens off in the distance, that was all he needed.

"Do you hear those sirens, Matherson? They're headed here. I guess we'll just have to run for it. Too bad about Anderson and McCormick."

Matherson looked with contempt at Shea and shook her head. "We're not going anywhere, asshole. I'd rather burn in hell than let them down. I'd suggest getting your rifle ready. Things may get hot."

Shea looked at her in disbelief. "Didn't you here what Anderson said? We have his permission to leave."

"I heard him. He gave us his permission, but he didn't order me to leave, so I'm not leaving. If you want to hoof it out of here, be my guest."

Shea wanted to argue the point, but the first cruiser had pulled in and Matherson opened fire. Without any other options, Shea joined her. The police clearly hadn't expected to be engaging a fully armored force with assault weapons. The two didn't have much problem keeping the police from getting out of their flitters. But more and more of them were arriving. Shea was beginning to worry that eventually he and Matherson wouldn't be enough to hold them at bay, when Anderson and McCormick emerged from the building. McCormick looked to be injured and Anderson, with Diaz's body over his shoulders, was helping McCormick get to the flitter.

When they reached the flitter Anderson tossed Diaz's body in and then helped McCormick in. "I thought I told you to leave if things got hot."

"Believe me, I wanted to," Shea said. "But, this bitch wouldn't leave you behind. Said she'd rather burn in hell than let you two down."

Matherson slammed the flitter into gear; the police scattered as it jumped forward. Several squad flitters followed. Anderson keep up a heavy fire with his TAZ.

Shea counted four flitters following. Enough of this shit, he thought, as he began lobbing grenades at the police flitters. They broke off the chase.

"We made it!" Shea exclaimed.

Anderson dropped his rifle and started to remove McCormick's armor. McCormick was no longer conscious. Shea could see that the wound was bad. Anderson stopped the bleeding and bandaged it. "We're going to need to get him to a hospital if he's going to make it," Anderson said to Matherson.

"We can't bring him to the hospital," Shea said. "The Consortium will find out who we are and then we're all dead."

"I'm not going to sit by and watch him die!"

"Sir," Matherson said. "Captain McCormick has a private regen tank and a staff doctor. I never understood why he kept such an expensive thing when he decided not to start up his merc outfit, but I guess it's just as well that he did."

Shea looked around his new flat. It was fucking gorgeous, marble and crystal everywhere. Several expensive paintings that a decorator ensured him were of the finest artistic quality hung on the walls. Even McCormick would be impressed with the flat. Shea's bank account had the right number of zeros, and there were two beautiful women asleep in his bed, but he didn't feel the way he had expected to. He'd just made enough money to ensure that he'd never have to work again. Somehow he'd expected to feel good about himself, superior, but damn it, he just didn't. Instead of enjoying his new-found wealth, he kept going over what Matherson had said to him. *"I'd rather burn in hell than let them down."*

Why was it driving him crazy? Why couldn't he find some peace and enjoy his money? He had two women in his bed, what difference did it make if some crazy bitch was willing to burn in hell for someone? It made a lot of difference, Shea suddenly realized. He'd always felt alone and alienated and he'd believed that money could change that. Now he had money and he felt even more alienated. Instead of celebrating, he was moping around his new place wishing someone would rather burn in hell than let *him* down. "This is fucking stupid," he said to himself.

Shea wanted to scream in frustration, but instead he picked up the phone and punched in the number for McCormick's security firm. Three minutes later he was talking with Anderson on the holo phone.

"What is it, Shea? I'm very busy right now."

"Rumor has it that you and McCormick are starting a merc outfit."

"What of it?"

"I want to buy in. I'd like to be an equal partner. I've still got most of my money from the heist."

"Have you lost your little mind?"

"No, Anderson, I *want* in."

"Why?"

"When you and McCormick went back into the compound, I tried to get Matherson to leave you behind and she wouldn't."

"This is supposed to mean something to me?"

"No, I guess not. You take it for granted that people are willing to die for you. I've never had that. Hell, I've never even had anyone willing to be inconvenienced for me. I want to be a part of that."

"You can't just buy into that kind of loyalty, you have to earn it. You have to be willing to lay down your life for it. If no one has ever been that loyal to you, I'd say it was because you've never been that loyal to anyone."

Shea nodded. "You're right, but I want to change that. Hell, I *need* to change that. Otherwise it'll haunt me forever."

"You're still not what I'd think of as a merc."

"You'll need some kind of tech support. That's where I'd come in."

"You do realize that if we did allow you in as a partner, McCormick and I would be able to outvote you any time we disagreed with you?"

"I'm really not worried about that."

"All right then, here's your chance to be a human being," Anderson said, breaking the connection.

A human being, that was it, Shea realized. He'd allowed himself, on some fundamental level, to be nothing more than a cyborg. He'd alienated himself. This was his first human act since getting the implant. It felt good.

CPSIA information can be obtained
at www.ICGtesting.com
Printed in the USA
FSOW01n0837041216
28150FS